D1339304

This ~~book is to be returned on or b~~efore
the last date stamped below.

FEB 00 I S

MAY 00 U P

SEP 00 C W

JAN 01 A N

APR 01 D R

AUG 01 D F

A N JUN 14

K O APR 15
G N SEP 15

1 6 MAY 2016

C Z JUN 19

K N JAN 22

M Y FEB 2002
D T MAY 2002

SEP 02 E

24 APR 2003
OCT 07 K N
C S FEB 17
A Z APR 18
B T DEC 18

12 JUN 2003
11 SEP 2004
- 8 JUN 2005
10 JUN 2005
K S OCT 17

D5 JAN 2005

=2 MAR 2006

OCT 06 C R

FEB 07 K S

JUN 07 A N

FEB 08 D O

B N JAN 20

C R AUG 12

G T DEC 12
B R MAY 13
M R SEP 13
B Z FEB 14

A S OCT 14

I S JUN 16

angus
district
libraries

U IAN 2000

BRACKENTHORPE

Circumstance brought Beth unwillingly to Brackenthorpe, but she was to love this beautiful home of the Haughton family. When war began, Laurence and Edmund Haughton declared themselves for the King, and Beth was staunch in her support of the Royal cause. Edmund Haughton; Jonas Hardcastle, Parliamentary soldier; and Roderick Moore, flamboyant Royalist, were men who deeply affected Beth in her determination to cling to Brackenthorpe. However, when the time of decision was reached, Beth found her choice infinitely easier than she had expected.

Books by Kathleen A. Shoesmith
in the Linford Romance Library:

AUTUMN ESCAPADE

KATHLEEN A. SHOESMITH

BRACKENTHORPE

Complete and Unabridged

LINFORD
Leicester

First published in Great Britain in 1980 by
Robert Hale Limited
London

First Linford Edition
published 1997
by arrangement with
Robert Hale Limited
London

British Library CIP Data

Shoesmith, Kathleen, A (Kathleen Anne), *1938–*
Brackenthorpe.—Large print ed.—
Linford romance library
1. Love stories
2. Large type books
I. Title
823.9'14 [F]

ISBN 0–7089–5177–5

Published by
F. A. Thorpe (Publishing) Ltd.
Anstey, Leicestershire

Set by Words & Graphics Ltd.
Anstey, Leicestershire
Printed and bound in Great Britain by
T. J. International Ltd., Padstow, Cornwall

This book is printed on acid-free paper

1

THE years of my early childhood were happy ones, spent as the beloved only daughter of the blacksmith and his wife in a small village in the western part of Yorkshire. Our humble home, built of the local stone, was no grander in design than the houses of our neighbours, yet, from the first, I judged us as a superior family. To me my father was a prince among blacksmiths. Not only was he vastly capable in his trade, he was also something of a scholar and was looked upon with awe tinged by envy by his fellow villagers.

My mother had, it appeared, married beneath her station. For a female, she was well-educated and could read and write. She could also cast accounts although our monetary dealings were of the simplest and did not give full scope for her admirable talents. It was she who had taught my father. She taught him well and he took pride in reading aloud from the Bible and Fox's Book of Martyrs. To the best of my knowledge no one else in our village possessed either book-learning or books. Our two heavy tomes had pride of place upon our library shelf and, when considered old enough, I too was taught to read them.

I never learned the location of my mother's former home, nor did I ever meet any of her relatives, save one sister — my beloved Aunt Nan, who came to the village on infrequent visits, causing all to marvel at the richness of her clothing. Despite this evidence of family wealth, I never once heard my mother yearn for a better life.

To me our home was a veritable palace. My father's smithy, an exciting domain smelling of hot metal, horses and general heat, opened from our one large living-room. My mother did her cooking on a hearthstone at the smithy end of the room. She had a huge three-legged cauldron and from an iron bar above the hearth hung all her pots and kettles.

In comparison with our neighbours we were indeed wealthy and I can recall envious remarks being made about the pane of real glass in our lower window and the homespun curtains hung there by my mother. Our loft, reached by a wooden ladder, was probably no grander than those of the other villagers. It was roughly partitioned into two sleeping-chambers. My parents had one and I slept alone in the other, lonely for the sisters I had never had. I believe the only thing which marred my childhood days was the lack of young companions.

My mother was a sweet and gentle person with a cloud of dark hair and a ready smile for me but I knew that the other women of the village judged her to be reserved and difficult to know. She never encouraged questions about her past life and, if I should word a childish query, neatly turned the talk to other matters. I remember her best as she sat in the firelight's glow on a winter evening, playing her hautboy to our singing, but I cannot remember the village people ever being invited to join us. In later years I wondered if my mother had sought this seclusion on my behalf.

When I was seven years of age, I had the first of what were to be many strange and frightening experiences. I had gone into the walled-in yard at the rear of the smithy to feed the fowls and suddenly and without warning my head began to throb with a pulsing rhythm. Bright flashes of pain seared my brow and I fell on to my knees, clutching at my ears to still a deafening clamour. As I knelt, my childish frame contorted with both fear and pain, a series of images began to flash past my inner eye.

When the vision finally left me, I tottered to my feet, terrified and spent. There my mother found me. When I began to sob out my tale within her sheltering arms, she stiffened, clapped a hand about my mouth and carried me bodily into the house, urging my nerveless legs up the ladder into my sleeping-chamber. She sat down with me on the stuffed straw mattress and ordered me to tell her everything.

Still frightened but more coherent now, I stammered an account of the pain, the drumming in my ears and those images — those dreadful images. When I fell silent I heard her give a long shuddering sigh.

"I wondered, my poor Beth," she whispered incomprehensibly. "There was an earlier occasion, child, and I *wondered* then!" Her voice was filled with anguish. "Oh, how I prayed that it would not be so! The first time was when, as a babe of two, you woke sobbing in your crib, saying aloud the name of your father's dog. We learned later that the poor beast had met an untimely end at that very moment when you cried his name. I

5

prayed it was naught but coincidence but now — "

Doubtfully I stared up at her.

"You mean it *happened*?" I whispered through dry lips. "What I just saw was *true*? No — it must not be true! I saw Aunt Nan and — and she *died*!"

It was three weeks before news reached us to verify the fact that my beloved aunt had died in childbed. Only she of my mother's family had ever kept a link with us. Now she was gone and would never again arrive at our door on her neat little mare with a groom in attendance and gifts in her saddlebag. Guilt lay upon my heart like a heavy weight. I was convinced that my poor aunt's death was in some way my fault. Sobbing, I demanded the truth of my mother and was partially reassured when she told me I had merely witnessed and not caused the tragedy.

"Ah, Beth," mourned my mother, "you will have this — this Dream again and again on your passage through life.

It is your curse, child, and could prove to be your downfall. Never speak of it except within our family and, even then, call it your Dream."

Though I did not understand, she would say no more, merely stressing that I must never speak of this frightening power that enabled me to have a secret vision of something veiled to other eyes. I said I would try to forget what had happened and said fiercely that I would never again permit myself an unnatural vision. My mother shook her head sadly and several weeks later, against my father's wishes, took me to see the swimming of a witch in the deep, fast-flowing stream outside our village.

"Look, Beth," urged my normally gentle and sensitive mother. "Look well and never forget this day."

Staring in stupefaction at the sight of an ugly, cursing crone, struggling in that torrent and secured by ropes held by men on the opposite banks, I wondered why my mother had forced me to see this horror. When the old woman was dragged back on to land she was no longer cursing, for she was dead. At this point, Mother led me away, saying quietly:

"Beth — the old woman was suspected of witchcraft and that is why she was swum today. Had she lived, they would have burned her as a witch. Because she did not swim she was judged innocent."

"Innocent?" I said chokily. "But they *killed* her!"

My mother gave me a long look.

"Strange old women are often thought to be possessed by wickedness," she said. "I had an aunt once. When her intended husband died on the eve of their wedding she became odd and solitary and cared for nothing save her two pet cats. We live in troubled times, child. Her strangeness was noted and folk accused her of witchcraft."

I wet dry lips with my tongue.

"Was she burned?" I breathed.

Mother shook her head grimly.

"They took her away to be swum, Beth, just like that old woman we have just seen. They found my aunt innocent too, for she drowned."

I drew in a shuddering breath.

"Why must I know all this?" I demanded, my voice rising in a sob. "It's the — the *Dream*, isn't it? It's *that* that makes you fearful!"

"Yes, Beth," she said sadly. "This Dream of yours is no new thing. It has been visited upon others of our family. The aunt of whom I speak was afflicted in this same way. She was unwise and spoke freely of what her visions showed. Even though things did not always come to pass exactly as she foretold, it was not long before the blame for every misfortune was set at her door. Always hold your tongue on what you know, child, for folk are always eager for a scapegoat."

"I will never speak of it to anyone," I vowed firmly. "*Never!*" Hopefully, I added: "Perhaps I will never have the Dream again!"

I was to find myself in its grip on many future occasions, however unwillingly, but my mother did not live to know this. She died of a fever within months of her revelation of what the Dream might hold in store. I held her poor wasted hand to the last and soon forgot all fear of unnatural visions in my childish grief.

Three years went by. My father and I lived happily enough together and I did my best to reconcile him to the loss of his beloved wife. Then, one chill October day in the year 1637, something occurred which robbed me of all that I had held dear. At the age of eleven years, I was uprooted from what was loved and familiar and was carried off into a new and alien existence.

Sometimes, as on that fateful day in October, travellers would halt at the forge to have their mounts shod. That day I had gone to the stream to the place where the best rushes grew. Our supply was low and rushes were needed for strewing on our packed-earth floor and for fashioning into rushlights for the coming winter. Autumn sunshine shone up the water. I set down my bundle of rushes suddenly, as I remembered the swimming of the witch. Shivering, I realised that this memory was unforgotten in every detail. Shaking my head fiercely to rid it of morbid thoughts, I was suddenly assailed by a sharp pain across my brow and my ears began to throb to blinding flashes of light. With a stab of helpless panic, I knew that the Dream was upon me again.

I came quickly to myself, to find I was kneeling perilously close to the rushing torrent of the stream. Tears stung my eyes and flowed down my cheeks as I turned and ran stumbling back to my home.

Gasping, "Father — my father!" I rounded the house only to stop abruptly. Two horses were in the smithy-yard. One was being gentled by a groom. It was a highstrung black with whitely rolling eyes. The other horse, an undistinguished mare, stood quietly by the anvil.

I could see a gentleman kneeling in the yard beside a fallen figure and I did not need to see that fatal wound on the beloved brow to know that my father had been struck by the hooves of the black horse. I knew he was dead. The Dream had revealed this and more, minutes ago, beside the stream.

I think I must have swooned for I next found myself inside the house, sitting on one of the carved-wood stools with my head held down. When I sat upright I saw the gentleman staring at me in evident sorrow and I glared back, my eyes filled with hatred.

"You have killed my father!" I told him bitterly.

His head bowed in assent and he did not attempt to excuse his action but the groom rushed into speech to explain that a dog had run into the smithy-yard, startling the high-bred horse into rearing and lashing out with its hooves.

"My name is Laurence Haughton," said the gentleman at length. He was of medium height, having brown hair flecked with grey, mild blue eyes and expensive-looking, if travel-stained, clothing. From the very depth of my being I hated his unfamiliar air of elegance and wealth. I scowled blackly at him as he went on: "This is a sad affair, child. I must contact your kin. What was your father's name? Did you live here alone with him?"

"His name is D-Daniel Gaunt," I said bleakly, suddenly too overcome to sustain hatred. "There is no one but him. I — I am called Beth and I have no other kin."

Mr Haughton stroked the neat beard that matched his hair for colour and exchanged a frowning look with his groom.

"Come, child," he urged. "You must have relatives! Tell me their names and I will apprise them of the situation. I am sure they will be glad to care for you."

I shook my head.

"There is no one," I insisted dully. "My mother is dead. I did have an aunt once but she died too."

By now dusk had fallen and my unwelcome visitors were muttering plans of staying on uninvited. I slept in my own room and I believe the gentleman used my father's. I was too shocked and weary to care.

Next morning I was kept indoors while arrangements were put in hand for the funeral. I paid little heed to proceedings for my anguish and hatred had been dissolved in mere apathy.

Mr Haughton and his groom stayed on for about a week. Questioning the village people brought only shaken heads. My family had kept aloof and no one knew much about us. At a loss what next to do, Mr Haughton made a sudden decision. He could not, he declared, in all humanity leave an eleven-year-old girl, orphaned at his hand, to fend for herself. No — he intended to take me with him. From now onwards his home was to be mine, his children to be brother and sister to me.

Little about this decision pleased me but the prospect of living alone with no means of support was even less inviting. There had never been talk at home of my taking up employment but it seemed that this was now to be my lot. I held no real belief that I was to be taken lovingly into Mr Haughton's family. He was a grand gentleman, the like of whose clothing I had never before seen and, from the little he told me of his home, it sounded a veritable palace. After much thought I told myself grudgingly that working in this gentleman's house must serve until something better offered itself to me.

Not unnaturally I was loath to leave behind the possessions which held all my happiest memories — especially the finer things which had been my mother's. But Mr Haughton was firm. I must take only what his empty saddlebags would hold. As he allowed me to pack these bags myself, I was able to cram in a set of pewter mugs and two candlesticks — my only signs of wealth. I also took all of my clothing, the heavy family Bible and my mother's hautboy — an instrument I could not play.

Regretfully, I looked at the furniture and the cooking utensils, then ran swiftly to our nearest neighbour who had been kind to me when my mother died. I gave her everything left within the house and she hugged me for the first time, her eyes filling with tears. For a weak moment I wondered if she could be persuaded into taking me into her own family. Then I stiffened my resolve. Mr Haughton had killed my father. It was only proper that he should feel responsible for my welfare.

★ ★ ★

I first saw Brackenthorpe Hall on a bright autumn day, with the trees in its park turning russet and gold in the sunshine. Mr Haughton's home was a

16

stone-built Elizabethan mansion with two large front wings and a central entrance. I had never seen anything so magnificent in the whole of my eleven years of existence and I fell instantly in love with my new abode with a passion that time was not to fade.

I was bone-weary and heartsick for my dead father and the brief joy occasioned by my first sight of Brackenthorpe was overshadowed by the unexpectedly inimical greeting of Mistress Haughton. In later years, I was to learn that her husband had not seen fit to acquaint her in detail with my circumstances and that she had drawn what was to her the obvious conclusion. On that first day I only knew that this hard-faced woman thought me an intruder and hated me accordingly.

I stood in the vastness of the hall, clutching tightly at Mr Haughton's hand, finding it impossible to smile at this woman he told me was to be a second mother. Swallowing hard, I stared at her still handsome features, at the faded fair hair drawn back severely from her harsh countenance. I saw the cold pale blueness of her eyes, the sharply etched frown marks on her brow, and miserably compared her in my mind with the dark-haired gentleness of my mother. Mistress Haughton made no attempt to greet me and the angry red patch high on each cheekbone warned that she did not intend to accept me gladly.

Elizabeth stood scowling at her mother's side, taking her cue from the older woman. But for her expression she would have been a pretty child but her lips drooped in a petulant manner and her eyes, of a brighter blue than her mother's, flashed scorn upon my homespun gown and the saddlebags at my feet. This child of nine with the fair angelic curls was the girl Mr Haughton had fondly believed I would call sister. Although I was to make an effort to like her, I was never successful and she never became my friend.

The Haughton's son was fifteen years

of age and thought himself a man. He favoured his father both for looks and for kindliness of nature. He made me welcome from the very beginning and but for his cheering presence I might have fled back to my old home and begged a home from my old neighbours.

To my surprise Mr Haughton did indeed try to treat me as a daughter and I found no tasks assigned to me. My small bedchamber opened from Elizabeth's and I was to share the services of her maid. But for the antipathy of Mistress Haughton I would have been truly content with my new life. The mistress must have misheard my name, I thought innocently at first, for she always called me Bessie. It did not take long for me to realise her mistake was intentional and meant to cause me discomfort.

Although I did not forget my past life or my beloved father time muted the sharpness of my sorrow. As for the Dream — *that* I would be happy to forget, for it had foretold tragedy on each occasion. I intended to heed my mother's advice of long ago. This strange power must remain my secret!

2

"I FEAR there is to be war with Scotland," said Mr Haughton gloomily on a rain-washed February day in 1639.

I had been an accepted member of the Haughton family for sixteen months now — accepted with warmth and consideration by Mr Haughton and Edmund and with chill resignation by Mistress Haughton and Elizabeth.

Edmund had not wished to go to university and at seventeen had already completed his education. His former tutor, Master Anthony, had been retained in order that he might continue to teach Elizabeth and me. Mr Haughton had made this decision on realising my aptitude with pen and figures and my quick grasp of the intricacies of the French language. So Master Anthony informed me one day — adding that he would have sought another post, had Elizabeth been his only pupil. He seemed to take great joy in teaching me and I knew I outshone the younger girl in all my studies with him. At needlework, dancing and performing upon the lute, however, I had to own that Elizabeth far surpassed me. As our teacher in these subjects — Mistress Haughton herself — disliked me unceasingly, perhaps my inaptitude was only to be expected!

On this grey February day we were all seated before a blazing fire in the hearth at one end of the great hall. The servants had erected screens to give the feeling of a smaller room but much of the heat escaped upwards into the high, vaulted roof of the hall.

Edmund was carving a hunting scene on a panel of wood. He had considerable skill with his hands. When his father spoke his knife stilled upon the work and he stared.

"War?" he echoed. "England against

Scotland? Surely not! Are you certain of this, Father?"

Laurence Haughton nodded sombrely and spread his hands.

"It is all a matter of religion," he explained. "The Scots drew up what they call a National Covenant against our English prayer-book and service. It seems they are now to go a step further and prepare to do battle with the King, on this and similar issues."

My eyes widened.

"With the *King*?" I breathed incredulously, leaning forwards upon my stool. "No one may fight the King! His power is ordained by God. We all know that!"

However we were vastly relieved to learn later that there was to be no war with Scotland — at least not yet. I strove to understand how it had all come about — how anyone could challenge the King's right. Edmund teased me and told me that if I were to grow into a proper lady I must not trouble my head with politics and such masculine matters. When I persisted he said that King Charles had asked Parliament to vote him money for his war with Scotland. In some unaccountable manner the members of Parliament had dared to defy their monarch and refused him the money. As theirs was the first Parliament for many years, surely it would have been sensible for them to accede to the King's wish and safeguard their own employment?

My birthday was in mid-April and I had been thirteen for less than three weeks when the King dissolved the foolhardy Parliament. However I had little interest now to spare for politics. Something had occurred which was nearer by far to my heart than the affairs of our King on his distant throne in London town.

I had come to look upon Edmund Haughton in the light of my champion and as more than a mere adoptive brother. He liked me well enough and never faltered in the kindness he showed to me and in my childish way I had *hoped* — My grey-green eyes were wide and clear and my brown hair curled without artificial aid yet I knew I could not claim to be a beauty. Even so, locked within my heart was a glow of hope that — one day — Edmund might view me with supreme favour and make me mistress of my lovely Brackenthorpe Hall.

Alas for girlish daydreams! No one had deemed it necessary to explain to me — the intruder in their home — that Edmund had been betrothed from his cradle days to a young lady of wealth and good family. This month we were to be honoured with a visit from Mistress Barbara Charlton's family and — before the year was out — we were to dance at her wedding with *my* Edmund.

Fortunately Elizabeth had never guessed at the secret plans I had woven for my future so there was nothing she might vent her spite upon on this occasion. Against all natural inclination I liked Mistress Barbara immensely and could have been her friend. She was a sweet-natured, gentle young lady of sixteen years and, try as I might, I could not hate her. Ah well — if Edmund had to be wed, then who better than she, I pondered, never pessimistic for long. Perhaps I could not have Edmund but possessing this house could still remain my dream! I was young enough not to judge this dream hopeless.

I had not experienced that other, terrifying Dream in all the time of my life at Brackenthorpe Hall. Sometimes, when I lay within the sheltering comfort of my bed-curtains, I thought of what had gone before. Although my parents and the Dream itself were clear enough memories a hazy mist seemed to separate me from the years of my early village life. Sometimes I found difficulty in recalling the smallness and the poverty of my former home. When I looked at the polished boards of my bedchamber floor and gazed upon the splendour of the linen-fold panelled walls, it seemd that here was where I had always belonged.

I resigned myself to think of Mistress Barbara in friendship and without envy and when we learned in October of that same year of her unexpected death I was as shocked and distressed as anyone else. It was only later that I pondered on the fact that Edmund now had no prospective bride before him.

In spite of our own comfortable conviction that there would be no war with Scotland His Majesty met and fought with the Scots and was defeated at a place called Newburn in the far north. Again the King needed money — this time to make *peace* — and again he called Parliament, which met in November of 1640.

We at Brackenthorpe needed something to divert us from the knowledge of sweet Mistress Barbara's death, so we fell to earnest discussion of the political situation. Mr Haughton subscribed to a news sheet, which was sent from

London, so we were well informed of our country's position although the intelligence usually reached us late, when matters had already taken a fresh turn. We read of Lord Strafford, a Yorkshireman and known by repute by Mr Haughton. He had served His Majesty well in Ireland and now was home in England to advise his King in these troubled times. We had scarcely learned this before another news sheet was brought. This one told us that Lord Strafford and Archbishop Laud of Canterbury had been arrested by Parliament on a charge of treason. They were now languishing in the Tower of London. In June of the following year Mr Haughton returned from a visit to London town to regale us with details of Lord Strafford's execution. When I protested that an earl should not have had to die in this manner Mr Haughton sighed and said: "Beth, my child, there is much you do not understand, despite your application and willingness to learn!

His Majesty did not wish for Strafford's death but there was a mob of people howling about the Palace of Whitehall for the earl's life. Rather than subject the Queen and his children to fear and torment by this mob the King was obliged to agree to the execution." He gave another heavy sigh and added: "If only we could be assured this was the end of it — but matters will not rest here. I fear only worse can follow."

Mr Haughton's gloomy prediction was echoed by an acquaintance of his who lived to the east of York. This Mr Jonas Hardcastle was a steely-eyed gentleman who took the astonished Mr Haughton to task for his unquestioning defence of our monarch. It seemed that Mr Hardcastle dared to hold the view that the King might stand in error!

The two gentlemen held a low-voiced but heated discussion beside the hearth of the great hall and I eavesdropped shamelessly from behind a screen until Mistress Haughton discovered my presence and whipped me with a birch rod for unladylike behaviour.

Both Elizabeth and I were well-used to these whippings and, when *I* was judged at fault, Mistress Haughton wielded the rod with venomous delight.

"You spying, inquisitive wench!" she hissed on this occasion.

Dragging me up to my room, she drew up my skirts and delivered several stinging blows upon my unprotected flesh. Elizabeth came quickly, eager to witness my disgrace. When she and her mother had left me, I flung myself face down upon my bed, bit hard on the back of my wrist to subdue a sob of pain and defiantly thought over what I had heard belowstairs.

Mr Hardcastle seemed — bewilderingly — to support not the King but Parliament: a mere body of men brought together by their King to do his bidding! To me this was a novel viewpoint upon our country's distress. Wide-eyed, I wondered if His Majesty could actually be wrong — then bit my tongue against what amounted to blasphemy. I had been taught that the King was answerable to God alone but the stern-faced Jonas Hardcastle dared to condemn and criticise his sovereign Lord. It all made little sense but troubled me greatly.

When later I confided my confusion in Master Anthony, the tutor did nothing to allay my fears. Although he took pains not to speak against his master I was uneasily aware that his opinion marched side by side with that of Mr Hardcastle, our visitor.

Still in need of clarification of a situation for which none of my experience could prepare me, I sought out Edmund.

I found him in the stables and he drew me down to sit upon a pile of straw in the dim warmth, put a brotherly arm about my shoulders and bade me begin. Scarcely had I uttered a dozen words than I realised that Edmund was not heeding me.

His arm had dropped from my shoulders to my waist and his other hand had strayed to the open neck of my gown. Lips close to my ear, he whispered unsteadily:

"Beth — you are so beautiful! Would that my father — "

I turned my head slowly to find his blue eyes very close to mine and his breath warm upon my cheek. His hold on me tightened and both of his arms closed about me. My heart thudded beneath the gentle swell of my still childish bosom as I took in the astonishing fact that Edmund Haughton found me beautiful.

There was a sudden stillness about him and I knew he was about to kiss me. With a soft, shy gasp of protest I pressed my face hastily against his shirt, only to feel his lips upon my neck.

"Beth — ah, Beth, this will not do!" he muttered all too soon and rose to his feet, drawing me up with him.

I was shocked by my reluctance to lose the warmth of his embrace and brushed the straw from my skirts in a sudden rush of embarrassment.

Edmund still held one of my hands in his and he lifted it to his lips in a manner which made me feel the equal of the finest lady in the whole of Yorkshire.

"Now that Barbara is dead, I am no longer betrothed," he said quietly. "Yet you came to us from nowhere, Beth, and I know that my mother would not like to think — "

This brought me speedily to my senses. Hastily I snatched back my hand.

"Your mother!" I gasped. "Oh — how she would whip me, if she ever learned of his little episode," I went on, my tone reflecting the bitterness inside me. "You are not yet of age, Edmund. You are too young to know your own mind. I am just poor Beth Gaunt, the blacksmith's daughter. Your mother sneers at me and calls me Bessie! Oh — Edmund, it just would not *do*!" I added in a whisper: "Yet, Edmund, I feel that I could love you — that I could belong here with you at Brackenthorpe for ever!"

Edmund bent and put his lips to my brow and when I looked up I saw his own youthful uncertainty.

"I pray that it may be so, Beth," he muttered and turned away to leave me.

Alone with the softly-breathing horses, I hugged my arms about myself and hugged also that secret knowledge that Edmund Haughton had been upon the verge of suggesting that we — he and I — might wed at some future, unconsidered date!

Soberly, I pondered on the many obstacles and differences in our status which would beset so foolish a goal. Edmund's family would never countenance a match for him with one such as me. Yet, I thought with warmth, nothing could quench my happiness on learning that Edmund did indeed favour me. Had I been less childishly bashful he would have kissed me lovingly. My own emotions had held us back. Possibly I felt myself to be overyoung to respond to his awakening ardour. Yet many girls little older than I were already married. Indeed it was legally possible for a girl to be wed at twelve years old and I was past fifteen.

Half-reluctantly I decided not to seek out Edmund so secludedly again — at least not yet. It would be unfair of me to face his youthful ardour with a repeated refusal. Making this decision, I found I could not now ask his opinion of Mr Jonas Hardcastle's odd championship of Parliament against our God-given ruler. If I could not speak of the matter privately with him, then I must hold my tongue on the score. To mention it when others were present would reveal that I had harkened all too well to my elders — by eavesdropping on their conversation!

Christmas was the usual festive occasion at Brackenthorpe Hall, with the giving of gifts, the singing of carols and the hanging of the kissing-bough in the great hall. The servants too joined in the merriment at this season.

The new year of 1642 had scarcely begun when we heard rumours that the possibility of war was with us again. In some bewilderment I protested that I had thought the trouble with the Scots was now past.

"Ah, if war should come, Beth," began Mr Haughton solemnly, "then it will be within our own boundaries — one faction against the other. This — ah — *quarrel* is no longer a Scottish-English affair."

I stared at him, not understanding.

"Can you mean that Parliament is to war with the — the King?" I demanded expecting him to deny this frightening prospect. "You think there could be fighting in England — between Englishmen?"

Elizabeth gave me a scornful look and took her father's arm possessively.

"Beth Gaunt — you are being silly!" she accused. "Father, tell foolish Beth that Parliament cannot fight the King.

She thinks she is clever but she has this tale wrong!"

Laurence Haughton gave his head a weary shake and I noticed there were now more threads of grey in the brown of his long, curling hair. He was ageing quickly, I thought regretfully.

"Little sister, you are the foolish one," rebuked Edmund, putting an arm about Elizabeth's shoulders to soften his words. "I am afraid Beth is right. War, if it comes, will be between supporters of Parliament and loyal subjects of His Majesty."

Mistress Haughton had been listening in silence and now she frowned and bade her daughter sit upon a stool beside her.

"Laurence — Edmund," she accused. "You are frightening poor Elizabeth. In any event war could never effect us up in the north. We are too far distant from Whitehall and the King. Depend upon it — there *will* be no war!"

Our next news sheet told us however that the King had left his palace and had gone first to Hampton Court and then to Windsor. Our uneasiness deepened and I saw the servants muttering together in worried groups, as rumours of war increased. I found I could not rely upon Mistress Haughton's conviction that we in Yorkshire would be safe from strife. Had not Lord Strafford been a Yorkshireman? Nothing had kept *him* safe. His life had not been preserved merely because he had hailed from our county! Mistress Haughton was being deliberately blind to the situation, I decided with all the wisdom of my fifteen years.

Yet even she became less confident there would be no war when news reached us that the King's wife, Queen Henrietta Maria, had set sail for the Low Countries. If rumour could be trusted she had taken all her jewels in the hope of selling them in Holland to raise money for the royal cause.

Landowners began to collect arms in preparation to fight and by now, said Edmund, fired with enthusiasm, every man in the country knew on which side lay his sympathies. To my mind no one of any importance could possibly choose to go against the King and speak in favour of Parliament. However Edmund told me I was quite wrong. Upon the side of Parliament were many strong-minded — and *wrong*-minded — noblemen, he said wryly.

It suddenly occurred to me how lucky I was to find myself in a staunchly Royalist household. How unhappy and unfortunate to have found myself among Parliamentary sympathisers! A further thought struck me. Had I been reared on other beliefs, perhaps at this moment I would be speaking for and not against the men of Parliament. It was very likely that circumstances and one's personal position chose sides in this promised strife, I thought profoundly.

I was preparing myself for bed on a freezingly cold January evening when an unexpected pain smote my brow and the Dream was upon me.

With terrifying clarity I saw a field strewn with dead and wounded men, rearing horses, fearsome knife-edged poles besmeared with gore and standards fluttering bravely over the shocking scene. The vision was brief and left me within seconds.

I was afraid now as I had never been before. Trembling, I climbed into bed and sat up against the pillows with the coverlet clutched about my shoulders. I was thankful for the bed-curtains, shutting me into my own safe, familiar world.

Shivering still, I tried to decide if my vision portended war to come. Always before, I had had my Dream of an occurrence already past. To have the power to view future events would be frightening indeed.

Vividly my shuddering mind portrayed that long-ago scene when the witch had been swum close to my village home. My mother had forced me to view the old crone's death as a warning of what might be my own fate should I ever reveal this strange power of mine. Could it be, I thought — colder even than the chill of January should make me — that I was indeed a witch? Mother's own aunt had been accused of witchcraft for speaking of her visions — which had been no worse than mine! She had died — which seemed an uncomfortable way of proving one's innocence.

With a sudden whimper of terrified protest, I burrowed beneath the bed-covering, gabbling the Lord's Prayer many times in rapid succession and finally I sobbed myself to sleep.

On the very next day Mr Haughton and Edmund lifted down the armour of their ancestors with great solemnity from its showplace on the walls of the great hall. I watched them from a distance, biting back a strong desire to scream that they must hurry. Last night had convinced me that war was almost upon us.

Under other circumstances the trying-on of that ancient armour would have been a huge jest and I would have laughed myself into a state of helpless hilarity. Yet even the sight of Edmund stumping round the hall in full armour like a large mechanical doll could not raise a smile from any of us — family or servants alike.

When Edmund stumbled and fell with a clamour of iron and muffled curses we merely hauled him to his feet, our faces anxious, and found no humour in the situation.

It was finally decided that only back and breastplates would serve from that motley collection of ancient metalwork. Mr Haughton also strapped on curved tassets to protect his legs. Edmund would have none of those, protesting that their ancestors must have fought at a snail's pace beneath that weighty welter of metal!

I rubbed my chilled hands together and only ceased to shiver when the armour was set aside. There had been so many fallen bodies in my vivid Dream. Would that none of them had been (or *should* be) of Mr Haughton and my dear Edmund, with his half-declared love of me.

Mr Jonas Hardcastle paid a further visit to Brackenthorpe and calmly told us of his intention to fight for the Parliamentary cause. Edmund, with a marked lack of tact, commented upon the visitor's ugly, close-cropped hair — a style new since we had last seen him.

"I choose to show I have done with the frills and frivolities of life, young sir," he said harshly. "Many who think as I do have made this outward show of our viewpoint."

"Oh," said Edmund blankly and sent a broad wink in my direction.

This did not draw even a smile from me. I was watching Mr Haughton and Mr Hardcastle and marvelled that they could discuss matters as mildly as they were now doing — and in calm and reasonable tones when it was so very obvious that they must now be sworn enemies. I despaired of ever understanding such men as these. How could they converse so amicably when within a short time they could be facing each other with drawn swords upon a bloody battlefield?

In the sanctuary of my own chamber that night I sobbed wretchedly for the stubborn, senseless determination of men who were set upon destroying each other — all for a quarrel started in distant London-town! Dabbing at my eyes with the sheet, I started when the bed-curtains twitched open. Elizabeth Haughton poked her head through the gap.

"Snivelling, are you, Bessie Gaunt?" she asked tauntingly. "I can scarcely sleep with your wailing! Surely you cannot be weeping to think that *my* father and *my* brother might be hurt in the fighting? They are nothing to you and *you* are less than nothing to them! If there is a war and they go off to fight, then I shall ask Mother to make you leave. You don't belong here, Bessie Gaunt! I think you must have bewitched poor Father into bringing you here, you blacksmith's brat!"

Her spite produced a quick return of my composure. Wanting to hurt her in turn, I put a complacent hand to my ruffled but naturally curling hair.

"Elizabeth, dear," I told her in honeyed tones. "I fear your right-hand curling-rag has come untied. If you do not attend to it, your hair will wear a lopsided look in the morning!"

She scowled at me and flounced off, closing our connecting door with a vicious bang. This interlude cheered me somewhat — a reflection upon my horrid nature, I supposed! I snuggled deeper into the warmth of my bed. There would be no war, I told myself comfortably. The King's quarrel with Parliament would soon be resolved. I smiled sleepily to myself. Poor Mr Hardcastle had cut off his hair to no effect! He should have kept his long locks and hidden the fact that he favoured a cause other than that of our monarch!

3

IN April Mr Haughton and Edmund prepared themselves for a journey to Hull, on the eastern coast. They rode off on my birthday — a fine, springlike day. I was now sixteen. Edmund sought me out to speak privately on the day before he left.

"We go to Hull, Beth," he confided quietly, "for His Majesty has hopes of securing this seaport. When the Queen returns from Holland we must be sure that she gains easy entry back into the country. I am convinced that this really *is* the beginning of full-scale war — although my father still holds to the hope that war will be averted. The Parliamentary faction are hard, determined men, of the like of Mr Hardcastle. Hull is a valuable port and they will not like to see it in the King's hands. I am telling you all this, Beth, just in case — "

Biting my lip, I put a hand on his arm.

"You are riding into danger, are you not, Edmund?" I asked him anxiously. "Do you fear there is to be fighting in Hull?"

"I just do not know, Beth," he confessed. "Now, listen to me. You recall that matter I broached last year, love?"

His tone warned me of what he was referring. I flushed and nodded, knowing he spoke of that incident in the stable.

"Yes, I recall it," I whispered.

"Tomorrow you are sixteen, Beth," he told me quietly. "I think you are quite old enough to know your own mind. You need not give me an answer yet. All I ask is that you will *consider* marriage with me — *if* I survive this promised war and *if* all objections can be countered."

"I will consider it, Edmund," I agreed, glad he was not pressing me for an immediate decision.

There were tears in my eyes when he took his farewell and I did not hide my face this time when he bent to kiss me.

Edmund was twenty now, a fine and upright young gentleman of moderate height and gentle manner. Already I knew I loved him a little and I grew cold at the thought of the war which might separate us permanently.

The gentlemen rode off and I was left to celebrate my birthday in solitary state. Mr Haughton had given me a gift of a length of green cloth of a light woollen material. Edmund had given me that parting kiss — the first I had ever received. Naturally enough I had received nothing at all from Mistress Haughton and Elizabeth — not even the customary birthday greeting. I refused to dwell upon Elizabeth's threat to have me sent away in her father's absence. Brackenthorpe Hall was my home. I had no other and it would take more than the ladies of this household to dislodge me!

My love of this attractive old house had never faltered. If I chose — in face of all opposition — to wed Edmund at some future date, then my position here would be assured. It was a tempting thought but I thought I owed Edmund at least a *heartfelt* decision. I must not agree to wed him just to gain Brackenthorpe!

He had shown me kindness from the very first and it would be unfair of me to use him in this manner. Grand, noble thoughts for a blacksmith's daughter, I thought wryly.

We had no news of either the King's attempt to take Hull or of our own gentlemen until the month of June. Those weeks had been uneasy ones for me, thanks to Elizabeth, but she had been unable to prevail upon her mother to bid me leave Brackenthorpe. I could not believe that Mistress Haughton had come to accept my presence in her home, so I assumed her reluctant to go against her husband's wishes in his absence.

I was in the stableyard on that June day, visiting Sorrel, the red-brown mare I sometimes rode, when a great black horse cantered in.

My first surge of eagerness died for the rider was neither Edmund nor his father. This man was a complete stranger to me. I watched curiously as he dismounted. We had had no visitors call here for quite some time and I wondered what he wanted with Brackenthorpe. He was enormously tall and seemed filled with a vitality which reached even across the yard to Sorrel's stall.

The stablemen rushed forward to care for the sweating, travel-stained horse and the man, with never a glance in my direction, strode off round to the main door. Giving Sorrel a final absent pat, I followed the stranger into the house.

As I entered he was just rising from a deep courteous bow to Mistress

Haughton and Elizabeth, his plumed hat held in one hand. There was both grace and flamboyance in his manner and I knew instantly that I had never before met his like.

His name, he announced, was Roderick Moore and I joined the group beside the empty hearth to learn more of him — ignoring Elizabeth's frown of dismissal. Mr Moore had come from Hull and he had brought a letter for Mistress Haughton from her husband.

She was just about to break the seal and read the letter when she noted my own undisguised interest. Rather than share its contents in my presence she pushed it into the pocket at her waist. Mr Moore must have been a very observant gentleman for his dark blue eyes with their ridiculously long lashes swivelled from Mistress Haughton to me. He raised a black brow and favoured me with a droll wink. Elizabeth saw him and she bridled and flushed an angry red.

The visitor waved a negligent hand

in my direction and said:

"I have met your charming daughter, Mistress Haughton. Pray give introduction to this other young lady."

There was a brief silence. Mistress Haughton stiffened and primmed her lips. I answered for her.

"I am Elizabeth Gaunt, sir," I told him, making my curtsey. "My friends call me Beth. Those who are not my friends have other names for me."

My tone of defiance would doubtless be rewarded by that spitefully wielded birch rod but for the moment I did not care. Mr Moore took my hand and bowed over it in courtly fashion, his blue eyes glinting wickedly, as if he allied himself with me against the Haughton ladies.

I warmed to this handsome, unusual gentleman and wished I could beg news of Hull from him. However Mistress Haughton's grim expression warned me that I had ventured far enough for one day.

Mr Moore must have read my

thoughts for with a keen look at *her* and a further smile for *me* he said:

"You will be eager for news of your husband, Mistress Haughton. Pray read your letter. I will entertain the young ladies with news from the port of Hull."

Giving a cold nod, she sat at a short distance from us and unfolded the letter.

"Mr Moore," I begged instantly, "did His Majesty take Hull?"

The visitor shook his handsome head.

"Alas, no," he told us. "Sir John Hotham, the governor of Hull, closed the gates and would not allow the King to enter. There is, it appears, a fine store of ammunition there. It must be intended for the Roundheads and not for the Royalists."

"Roundheads?" echoed Elizabeth. I thought she spoke less from interest than from a need to draw his attention. "What are Roundheads, sir?"

He smiled at her.

"It is a name that has been given to some of the Parliamentarians, Mistress Elizabeth," he explained. "In the main, our enemies wear their hair in the normal manner but the Puritan faction have had their locks close-cropped in disapproval of vanity. Therefore they have been named Roundheads or sometimes 'crop-ears'."

Mr Hardcastle must be a Puritan, I thought, then dismissed this side-issue.

"But — the King's aim?" I demanded impatiently. Unimportant details did not matter. "How may the Queen enter the country again if Hull is unsafe for her?"

Mr Moore gave me a considering look from his dark blue eyes.

"Mistress Beth," he said, with a shake of his head, "I pray you keep a watch on your tongue."

I flushed with chagrin to receive even so mild a rebuke before Elizabeth.

"Is it not common knowledge, sir?" I murmured. "Then I am sorry! But this is a Royalist house. We have no enemy here and we may speak freely."

He shook his head.

"When war comes, Mistress Beth," he said, "we will be hard-put to recognise friend from foe." Then he smiled. "Never fear — the Queen will gain entry in some manner or other. She is a very determined lady!"

Mistress Haughton joined us beside the hearth. She was frowning uncertainly. Tapping the letter in her hand, she said slowly:

"My husband writes that war is now a certainty. He lists the servants and tenants he requires to join him and says I am left in full charge with only old Jacob and Master Anthony being the men to remain amongst us. I cannot like this, sir!" she finished coldly, to the bearer of the tidings.

Roderick Moore gave a wry shrug.

"Strange times are before us, ma'am," he warned her. "I go next to arrange matters at my own home, which lies north of here. My lady mother is many years your senior and may find herself in harder case. Yet what can loyal subjects of the King do — save take up arms on his behalf? We have no choice, ma'am, and nor have you — except to do your husband's bidding."

His tone was cool with rebuke and Mistress Haughton reddened angrily.

"When do you go to your own home, sir?" she asked.

Her tone was far from hospitable and I winced inwardly. After all, Mr Moore had ridden many miles in order to deliver her husband's letter. She should not show discourtesy merely because the war seemed about to cause her personal inconvenience. Apparently, Elizabeth shared my views — an unheard of occurrence — for she pointed out hastily to her mother that both Mr Moore and his horse would be in need of rest before they travelled further north.

"I will bed down in the stable beside Fury if no room is available," suggested our visitor with a restrained lack of expression.

56

Belatedly recalling the fact that her husband would be incensed should she refuse hospitality to his messenger — who was possibly also a good friend — Mistress Haughton arranged that he should take the empty bedchamber next to Master Anthony's. That was only proper, she said primly, in a house full of ladies.

That evening, after our meal, we sat in the great hall and Elizabeth performed for us upon the lute, singing to her own accompaniment. She had a sweet, true voice and I kept silent, knowing I would not be asked to play. I could not compete with her musically and did not begrudge her this moment of minor glory. Politely Mistress Haughton asked Mr Moore if he would like to play for us. She seemed to have regretted her earlier incivility and was now treating him with guarded politeness.

"I do not play the lute, ma'am," said the guest with a smile, "but I have been told that I am passing fair upon the hautboy!"

Eagerly I broke through her regrets that there was no such instrument in the house.

"I have one, sir!" I said, rising to my feet. "It was my mother's. I pray you will play it for me!"

I ran from the room before Mistress Haughton should forbid me. When I returned Mr Moore took the instrument from me gravely, then set to piping a lively air, to which we tapped our feet beneath our gowns. (I was wearing my new gown, made from Mr Haughton's birthday gift.) Then Elizabeth rose and danced gracefully in time to the tune. Spontaneously I applauded and won a rare smile from her.

I contrived to be in the stableyard next day when Roderick Moore made preparations for departure.

"Sir," I said softly, "when do you think this war will begin? I — I am afraid for Mr Haughton and for — for Edmund."

"You show more interest than those

two within doors, Mistress Beth," he said, with a lift of a dark brow.

I bit my lip.

"I have no kin of my own," I murmured in explanation. "When my father died Mr Haughton brought me to live here at Brackenthorpe. He treats me as a daughter, you see, and has become dear to me."

"*They* have no love for you, little Beth," he said suddenly, pausing in the act of tying his cloak across his mount's saddle.

"Mistress Haughton and Elizabeth have never really accepted me into their home," I said briefly. "It does not matter, sir, for I am well-used to their dislike."

"Had you been a boy, I would have bidden you leave them and come a-soldiering with me, little Beth!" he smiled. "I like your spirit! However, you must stay here with these who do not love you. Mr Haughton will obey his King and be from home henceforth. I cannot yet say when war will be declared. Already, the King and Parliament are sending out their orders for the support of men and ammunition. In the main, I believe Yorkshire will speak in favour of his Majesty. Now, my little politician — you are as well-informed as I!"

He kissed my hand in farewell, then rode off, raising his arm in a salute as his black horse carried him out of sight.

In the sanctuary of my own room I held to my cheek the hautboy played last evening by Mr Moore and I sighed. I had liked this Royalist gentleman immensely! With men such as he upon his side the King could not fail to succeed.

I had never before seen a man as handsome as Roderick Moore. Yet he did not seem unduly concerned with his own looks. His coat had closely fitted his strong wide shoulders and I had a feeling that a man of steel lay beneath his flamboyant exterior.

No one would ever need to fear for his safety as I feared for Edmund's.

Edmund Haughton lacked the height, looks and elegance of Mr Moore but Edmund was loved and familiar and it was wrong of me to compare the two of them. Mr Moore had gone and it was unlikely we should ever meet again. Edmund was *mine* — if I wanted him — and with him would come my beloved Brackenthorpe. Indeed there *was* no comparison between them! Roderick Moore was merely a passing stranger who had appealed to my imagination. He would soon be forgotten.

I must have only imagined that Elizabeth was softening towards me. Her friendlier manner before Mr Moore had not deceived him and should not have deceived me. On the day after his departure I discovered that my hautboy was missing. I soon found it. It was lying in a corner of my room. Although it had been fashioned of extremely hard wood it was now battered and useless. Elizabeth must have used considerable force to destroy the instrument Roderick Moore had played so well. For several days she darted me eager, expectant looks but I held my tongue and did not accuse her. My old life was now so far behind me that she had not hurt me as she had probably hoped when she spoiled this memento of my mother.

For all the fact that I had stressed to Mr Moore the kindness of Mr Haughton I still sometimes thought of the violence of my father's death at his hands. Obviously some parts of my old life were not forgotten — or forgiven — and I knew I was capable of bearing a grudge. The Haughton family owed me a debt! I would be foolish if I refused Edmund. By marrying him I would make my position at the Hall unassailable for all time.

Yet unaccountably this course lacked attraction for me and I wondered at myself. Surely the Royalist visitor had not impressed me to such an extent that he could overshadow both my feelings for Edmund and my avowed ambition that Brackenthorpe should be mine?

4

MR HAUGHTON and Edmund arrived home at the end of August to find that the crops of the tenants' farms had already been harvested. The month had been unseasonably wet but it seemed that nothing could damp the fervour of the Haughton gentlemen for their King's cause.

I was with the family beside the hearth of the great hall to hear the latest news. Our country was now officially at war. This much we had learned even before the gentlemen removed their travel-grime.

"We have come straight home from Nottingham," reported Mr Haughton soberly. "His Majesty has many loyal subjects in that district and others, such as we, travelled to be there at the formal declaration of war."

I gave an inward shudder as that unhappy battle scene from the Dream flashed upon my mind. Edmund noticed my distress and put a comforting hand upon mine. Although she made no comment his mother's brows came together in a black frown and I guessed I would receive the length of her tongue later. In the presence of her husband and Edmund she was always less noticeably cold towards me.

"The declaration was made on the twenty-second day of this month," continued Mr Haughton in suitably subdued tones. "It was a cold, wet day. We watched the raising of the King's battle-standard with rain pouring down upon us. The standard had been made specially for this occasion and no less than twenty men were needed to hold it steady."

"Were the royal children there?" demanded Elizabeth, eager for lighter details.

"Prince Charles was there," put in Edmund. "He is a well-grown lad, for all he is only twelve. The King's nephew from Germany was there too. His name is Prince Rupert and he is a renowned soldier. Although it was so wet we learned later that no less than eight hundred foot-soldiers and three hundred horse-soldiers were present, as well as all the nobles and gentlemen."

"It must have been an awesome sight," I said wistfully. "Would I had been there to see it!"

Mr Haughton smiled at me.

"I must admit I was quite affected by the whole affair," he said. "When the standard was up and the King's message had been read by a herald we all shouted 'God save the King' and flung our hats up in the air. Aye — it was a moving occasion!"

Mistress Haughton had been silent until now. She frowned and said:

"What comes next? We have managed the harvest without you but I cannot say how we will fare when you are gone — and have taken all the men with you."

"You will have Master Anthony, old Jacob and perhaps young William," her husband told her firmly. "The rest must accompany Edmund and me. The King is now engaged in a tour of recruitment and so, I fear, is our parliamentary enemy. We in the north, I am proud to say, are declared for His Majesty. We go beneath his own command."

His wife took no pride in this assurance.

"Aye — but *when* do you go?" she demanded.

Laurence Haughton gave a sudden sigh.

"We leave soon to join the King's army," he said. "I imagine we are to march on London."

I repressed an inward shudder.

"I am sure *you* do not need to go, Father," said Elizabeth coaxingly. "They will do well enough without your help. We need you here," she added, with a side-glance for her mother's approval.

"Hush, little sister!" chided Edmund. "Would you have us to stay at home and hide behind your skirts?"

"No one would know!" retorted Elizabeth. "But you will not listen to me, will you? You are set on leaving us. It is not fair!"

I did not wish them to leave either but hoped my own reasons were less selfish than those of Elizabeth. Not once had she expressed the fear that these, her dear ones, might perish on the field of battle!

When faced with orders from Mr Haughton, the tutor Master Anthony, shook his head and said politely enough but firmly that he was leaving Brackenthorpe. Incredibly, he intended to volunteer for the parliamentary army. Two of the stablemen left with him and I know that their master was astounded to find his wishes so thwarted. It seemed that this war was removing proper respect from the servant-class. Until he left the house Master Anthony was in dire disgrace but he had been my friend and I could not let him go without bidding him farewell.

"Oh, but you have chosen wrongly," I told him sorrowfully. "Master Anthony, you are a wise and good man and yet you will not support your King. I cannot understand you at all, sir!"

He gave me a smile which was tinged by sadness.

"You have been an apt and thoughtful pupil, mistress," he told me quietly. "Surely you have the wit to acknowledge that all men — even poor tutors — must hold the right to their own opinions. I must stand firm to my own conviction — whatever the cost. Try to forget the myth that the King's power is God-given, mistress. Think of him instead as one despotic ruler who will not take counsel from wiser men. Ah, times are changing! I fear that much unhappiness lies ahead for us all. In some families, even fathers and sons are divided in their sympathies."

He left without attempting to seek a word with his late employer and

I wished him well from the bottom of my heart. Although I judged him foolishly wrong-headed I knew he was basically a good man.

Mr Haughton charged his wife to care well for his two daughters and I knew he was warning her to treat me fairly in his absence.

He and Edmund had brought home buff-coats to wear beneath their armour. They rode off with these sleeveless leather garments and their back-and breast-plates, packed with their other baggage in care of the servants accompanying them.

We had no word for over two months but were not unduly concerned as we had been warned of this likelihood. From various sources we received snatches of information about how the sympathies of the country lay. Passing travellers or a well-delayed news sheet told us tantalisingly little of what we longed to hear. It seemed that support for His Majesty came mainly from Wales, the south-west, the western Midlands and our own loyal Yorkshire. Parliament's cause seemed most favoured in the south and east of England, with a concentration upon London. Yet even this information told us little for we learned that supporters of the rival causes were to be found in areas declared for the opposing side.

Regrettably the Navy had sided with Parliament, one royalist gentleman told us. Indeed only one ship remained loyal to the King and only Newcastle and King's Lynn were Royalist-held as seaports.

Roderick Moore paid us a breif visit. He had hoped to join the King's forces together with Mr Haughton and Edmund but they had left us a week before he arrived. It seemed he had not yet officially enlisted his services and was considering going further south to join Prince Rupert's army.

"The Prince is renowned for his cavalry tactics," said Mr Moore, as he packed a parcel of food from the Brackenthorpe kitchens into his saddlebag.

I had contrived to be attending to Sorrel when he came to the stables. My presence there could not have seemed odd, I told myself, because the depletion of our outdoor staff meant that my help was sometimes needed. I believed I must have inherited my love of horses from my blacksmith father. In any case, I found it pleasanter to give help in the stables than to be at Mistress Haughton's beck and call within doors.

Mr Moore's highstrung black was prancing to be off on its way but I stroked its neck and calmed it into stillness. Suddenly a strong brown hand set itself on mine as I gentled the horse.

"Promise me that you will not lose your spirit, Mistress Beth," said Mr Moore softly. "Laurence and Edmund are here no longer and it is clear that Mistress Haughton has no love for you. Keep in good heart!"

"She will beat me occasionally," I admitted, "but I think she will not dare to send me away for fear of rousing her husband's displeasure. I will do well enough, sir. You must not fear for me. I love Brackenthorpe. Just *being* here is enough to make me happy!"

His concern warmed me and I ventured to pry a little into his own affairs.

"Sir — how did you leave your lady mother?" I murmured. "Will the care of your home be a great charge upon her?"

Mr Moore smiled.

"She would like you, Mistress Beth," he said thoughtfully. "Her spirit is like to yours. I know you would deal well together." He hesitated, then added: "Should matters go ill for the Haughtons she would be happy to receive you at Moorend. It is a fair journey from here but you have a horse and I am sure you would find that riding beyond Skipton town would not defeat you!" Ignoring my question as to what he thought *could* go ill with my adoptive family, he went on: "Moorend's situation can be discovered at any inn in Skipton."

I eyed him gravely, then dropped a curtsey.

"Sir — you are most kind," I said. "I do appreciate your goodness more than I can say but — Brackenthorpe is my *home*. I intend to stay here — come what may!"

He carried my hand to his lips.

"Brave words, Mistress Beth!" he applauded. "I hope that the safety of Brackenthorpe may remain assured but in these troubled times nothing is certain. I merely sought to offer you a refuge, should the worst occur." He quirked up a black brow and said very definitely: "I must go now, but we shall meet again, Beth Gaunt — depend upon it!"

He mounted his horse in one lithe spring, wheeled about and was gone. Staring foolishly after him, I was

74

dismayed to find that my eyes were wet with tears.

"Fare you well, sir!" I whispered beneath my breath. "Ah — fare you well!"

* * *

With fewer servants at her disposal to run the household, it was only natural that Mistress Haughton should detail more menial tasks to her daughter and to me. Yet, where Elizabeth found herself comfortably mending linen before a warm hearth, I discovered that my duties lay mainly in the kitchen regions and in the tending of the herb-garden, as well as the work I did in helping in the stables. Although never actually disobeying her husband in his stricture to care for me, Mistress Haughton ensure that my days were filled with wearying tasks. I fell exhausted into my bed on many an evening with the words "Bessie Gaunt, pray do this — " ringing in my ears like a sonorous church-bell. There was little tangible that I could protest about yet steadily my position in the house was changing.

At least I stayed reasonably untroubled within the sanctuary of my own room but it irked me still that I had to go through Elizabeth Haughton's chamber to gain entry. She had grown more spiteful of late, doubtless resenting the fact that her leisure hours had been curtailed. She was attempting to turn me into her maid, for the girl whose services we had once shared had left for the parliamentary cause together with her sweetheart, who was one of the defecting stablehands.

"Bessie — pray mend this torn ruffle," was one of Elizabeth's many ways of showing me my place.

However I told her quietly that I was too occupied with my own indoor and outdoor tasks to wait upon her. As I pointed out *she*, not I, was sewing-maid!

I knew that she reported all of

our conversations to her mother but I did not care. There were not enough hours in the day for me to serve two mistresses. I had put aside my fear of Mistress Haughton, for I was nearing seventeen years of age. It seemed certain she did not intend to rid herself of my presence in her husband's absence although her dislike of me seemed to have grown even greater. I had not felt her birch rod quite so often recently but her tongue gave vent to bitter words when I raised her ire. It was lamentably easy to anger her! Speaking of the war; hoping Mr Haughton fared well; using Edmund's first name — these remarks and many more drew her fierce attention to my head. Sometimes I wondered if she were trying to make me leave of my own will. Remembering Mr Moore's kindly-meant offer, I knew I could always go to his mother if life here proved unendurable. *Unendurable*, I thought in the next breath, Brackenthorpe — unendurable? Brackenthorpe was everything to me! I would never leave here willingly!

Fleetingly, I pondered on our royalist visitor. I wondered if he had a wife. Surely he would not have invited me to seek refuge with his mother, if he was wed? I told myself firmly that it was no affair of mine. My destiny lay here at Brackenthorpe and if becoming mistress here meant marrying Edmund Haughton — then marry him I would! The attractions of Roderick Moore meant nothing to me!

Firmly I catalogued Edmund's virtues. He was kind and gentlemanly and he loved me a little already. What more could anyone wish for? Mr Moore was admittedly handsome but he was sometimes harsh-spoken. In all probability he was braver than Edmund and might make a more dedicated soldier. Yes, I supposed him admirable in many ways but he was *not* for me. It would serve me well not to think so often of him. Why must I dwell so broodingly on the few occasions on which we had met?

I wondered if he would eventually meet up with the Haughtons and fight at Edmund's side, though he had spoken of joining the army of the King's nephew from Germany instead. In spite of myself I found I was praying for Mr Moore's safety as fervently as I prayed for Edmund and his father. All three had shown me kindness and I knew I would be desolated to learn that any of them had perished in battle.

The Haughtons had taken swords lovingly cleaned and polished by Elizabeth and myself. These same weapons had adorned the walls of the great hall, as had the armour, for many years — indeed since the time when the Haughton ancestors had gone to war. Edmund had spoken also of muskets. I knew nothing at all of firearms but guessed with a shudder at the damage they might cause. According to Edmund, a musket was a form of heavy pistol and loading one was a slow business.

Thinking of weapons sickened me and I bent over the herb-garden, attacking the weeds fiercely to blot out that vision of warfare that had once been mine.

"Mistress!" called a shy voice, startling me so that I pulled out a root of sage instead of the intended daisy.

I rose and brushed the earth from my hands, to smile at William, younger of our two remaining menservants. He was an obliging enough lad but was low in intellect — which was why Mr Haughton had not taken him to battle. Poor William would never have made a soldier. Just now his duties ranged from the stableyard to the milking-shed to the kitchen and he worked with cheerful effort at them all.

"Yes, William?" I enquired, pushing back a curling tendril of hair. "Does Mistress Haughton require me within doors?"

"Nay, mistress," he told me, "but go you in an' rest. 'Tisn't right that you should work so. Happen 'tis *my*

80

job — weeding an' such. I know herbs, mistress, so never fear I'll spoil t'herb-patch!"

Gladly I relinquished my task and bestowed a grateful smile upon William. I wondered if he had thought this out for himself or if the other servants had noticed how hard Mistress Haughton was making me work. My back was aching from my toil and I had broken a fingernail with my grubbing in the earth.

"You are a good boy, William!" I told him warmly.

He beamed and flushed to the roots of his lint-fair hair. Although several years my senior he did not resent being named "boy".

"You're a right good lass, mistress," he said, as he bent his head over the herbs.

"Finished already, Bessie?" greeted Mistress Haughton's voice as I tried to slip unnoticed up the stairway to my own room. "Good," she went on, "I require you in the still-room. My

81

daughter and I are preparing potions and medicines. It has occurred to me that we should be ready to help injured soldiers at some later date. As you seem to be unoccupied, Bessie, you may help us — unless you would prefer to tear up an old sheet and roll bandages. They too may be needed."

I eyed her suspiciously, never trusting her when she was amiable towards me. Always hoping for a better relationship with the ladies of the household, I said I would be glad to assist with the potions. Within minutes I wished I had chosen bandage-making! Every odorous and unpleasant ingredient was assigned for *my* handling. Elizabeth's fair hands touched nothing more repulsive than the petals picked from last summer's roses!

However we worked well enough together and even Elizabeth seemed less spiteful as we stoppered the medicines and labelled the jars and bottles.

When a sudden pain stabbed my brow I winced and rose to my feet, a hand across my eyes.

"I — I have a headache — " I began faintly.

"Are you ill, Bessie?" demanded Elizabeth, backing from me in alarm. "I pray you will keep your infection to yourself!"

Heeding neither her words, nor Mistress Haughton's harsh grip upon my arm, I staggered from the still-room and dropped to my knees painfully on the stone floor.

"No — no!" I moaned, pressing my hands to my ears, sufficiently conscious on this occasion to attempt to fight the Dream. "The battle! Ah — *no*! Look — there behind you — !"

My voice failed and I keeled over in a dead faint.

When I came to my senses I was seated on a stool with my head pushed firmly down. My first thought was that this had happened to me before. *Then* I was eleven years old and had swooned at my father's death. My comforter had been Mr Haughton. *Now* I was past sixteen and Mistress Haughton, digging hard fingers into my neck, offered no comfort.

With an effort I shook off her hand and stood up unsteadily.

"I am sorry," I began, at a loss how to explain what had happened. "I believe I fainted."

Mistress Haughton was subjecting me to cold scrutiny and at the back of her pale eyes lurked something suspiciously like *fear*. How must the Dream's possession of me appear to an onlooker, I wondered anxiously.

"Bessie Gaunt," she said slowly. "Can it be that you take *convulsions*? Surely we would have discovered this before now? For a moment I judged you demented! What did you mean by that cry of 'battle'? I vow I thought you crazed — or bewitched."

I shuddered at her final word, then attempted a smile for Elizabeth, who was gazing at me from round, frightened eyes.

"Battle?" I said with a frown. "Are

you sure I did not say 'bottle', ma'am?"
I managed. "After all, I have been
stoppering potions with you this past
hour or more. I was attacked by so
violent a headache that I babbled
nonsense. I pray you will pay it
no heed and forget. Forgive me for
alarming you both."

I waited for Mistress Haughton's
reaction. Fear was still in her eyes
and I felt uncomfortable rather than
triumphant that I should have had the
power to make her afraid.

"Go to your room, Bessie," she
murmured at length. "You are in need
of rest. I fear your over-diligence at
your duties has tired you more than
was realised. My husband will not
wish to find you ill when he returns."
Her expression resumed its normal
bitterness as she added: "For some
reason or other, he has a fondness
for you."

Escaping with relief from her hard
eyes and Elizabeth's half-frightened
curiosity, I fled to my room and

flung myself upon the bed. I stared upwards, wide-eyed and tearless at the canopy over my head.

How could I begin to explain to the Haughton ladies that I had just experienced a terrifying vision? The Dream had come upon me with even less warning and greater clarity than was usual and they had been present to observe my helplessness when in its grip. Mistress Haughton had thought me demented or — bewitched.

With a sob I rolled over and buried my face in the coverlet. Let it not be true, I implored. Say he is alive! The Dream had been brief, its message stark. I had seen Roderick Moore charging into battle on his black horse, sword held aloft. There had been no doubt as to his identity. I had witnessed him struck from behind by a fearsome long pole with a knife-end and I had come to my senses judging him dead.

I drew up my knees and hugged them, weeping unconsolably.

"Roderick! Oh no — not Roderick!"

I moaned in agony, using his first name as if it were natural that I should do so.

A little later, I rose stiffly from my bed and splashed cold water upon my cheeks from my washbowl. My royalist friend, Roderick Moore, was dead. He had been killed in battle and I would never see him again. I knew that I had to accept this as truth. The Dream had never played me false.

Nothing seemed to matter any longer. Even if Mistress Haughton had gone further with her half-formed suspicions and called me *witch* it would have meant little to me. Roderick Moore had perished in battle and his passing left me totally bereft.

5

TWO weeks went by, then news began to arrive of a battle which had taken place in Warwickshire. The parliamentary army, led by the Earl of Essex, had met the King's army on the twenty-third day of October. According to rumour, by six o'clock in the evening fighting had ceased, leaving thousands of men lying dead on the battlefield.

My Dream had told me true. My vision of Roderick Moore being struck down had appeared to me on the exact day of the battle. Shuddering anew, I tried to turn my thoughts to other matters. Yet nothing seemed to hold my attention for long. I went about my daily tasks — fewer since the Dream — in dry-eyed stony silence. Fortunately no one was sufficiently interested to remark upon my air of shocked distraction.

Towards the middle of a damp, foggy December Mr Haughton and Edmund arrived home. Both were uninjured although they had had their first taste of battle. I waited in a sick agony of distress for them to describe the manner of Roderick Moore's death — which must be known to them.

They spoke of the battle at Edgehill in Warwickshire, in which they had fought with His Majesty's army. Neither of them made any reference to Roderick.

"But — who *won* the battle?" demanded Elizabeth when her father fell silent. "Neither of you look particularly elated! Surely you have not come home to tell us that the King's cause is lost?"

Edmund gave a wry shrug.

"In truth we are unsure which side won the battle of Edgehill," he admitted. "It seems that each has decided to claim victory! There were heavy casualties on each side."

Mistress Haughton frowned.

"Well, you are home again," she observed. "If this war is now over — what has been achieved, pray?"

Her husband shook a weary head.

"The *battle* is over," he informed her quietly. "I fear it was but the first of many. The *war* has scarce begun."

"Do not say you will leave us to fight again?" demanded his wife incredulously. "Why — it is almost impossible to run the house with the few servants you left us! I cannot but feel that you would do best to remain at home, from now onwards! Surely home and family must be set above all else?"

"You know nothing of the matter, Cecilia!" retorted Mr Haughton with scant regard for courtesy. I realised his feelings must have been strong for him to have thus rebuked his wife before us all. "Edmund and I must leave again to do our duty — the moment the King has need of us. There is no more to be said on the matter!"

His son gave him a considering look.

"I had not expected a battle to begin as this one did," he said, filling in an awkward pause. "We made camp on the top of Edgehill for the night and moved to the lower slopes at first light. We wore red sashes to distinguish ourselves from the enemy — who wore sashes of orange." He glanced at his father, who appeared to have recovered his normal calmness of manner, then went on: "It was well into the afternoon before a move was made. I think the waiting set us all on edge! It was the worst part. I believe we were all glad when Prince Rupert's cavalry charged and the battle began in earnest."

His father intervened at this point.

"I think you have gone far enough, Edmund," he said mildly enough. "The ladies do not wish for details."

"Indeed, no!" agreed Elizabeth. "Pray, did you see Prince Rupert? Is he vastly handsome — this nephew of the King? Was his brother there too — Prince Maurice?"

Conversation took on a lighter tone

and I sat with clenched hands, nails digging into my palms. Would they *never* speak of Roderick Moore? I knew I could not bring myself to enquire of him.

Eventually Mistress Haughton, ill-pleased by the promise of her husband's further absence from home, said suddenly:

"Did young Mr Moore meet up with you, Laurence? He arrived here a week after your departure. We gave him a night's lodging, of course."

My throat went dry as I waited for her husband's reply.

"We heard he had joined Prince Rupert's cavalry," nodded Mr Haughton. "After the battle we rode for London with the King but were turned back and so came home. Where the Prince's army went next, I cannot say." He hesitated then added: "There was a vast casualty-list at Edgehill."

I waited, sick at heart, for the official announcement of Roderick's death. Elizabeth gave an affected little scream.

"Oh, Father! Are you trying to break the news that poor Mr Moore has perished. Beth and I would be *devastated* to hear that, would we not, Beth?" she asked me, her blue eyes wide.

I returned her look levelly and murmured that it would indeed be a shocking thing to hear that an acquaintance of the family had been killed in battle. I marvelled that my voice should be so steady before the eyes of Edmund and his family. Inwardly I was weeping for the man who had so lightly declared we would meet again. There would be no further meetings between Roderick Moore and poor Beth Gaunt.

Yet I was to be proved astonishingly and joyously wrong in my assumption. We were in the midst of our Christmas preparations when the man I mourned and supposed dead rode up to Brackenthorpe and begged for a night's lodging.

He ate with us at table and I scarce

consumed a morsel of food for my eyes were fixed upon him. I was foolishly convinced that he would vanish away should I dare even to blink. My heart was so full that I could not even bring myself to speak to him.

Talk was quite irritatingly general and the meal was almost over when the battle was mentioned.

"How did you fare at Edgehill, Mr Moore?" asked Edmund. His tone held polite interest but I could tell that he had no particular liking for the visitor and this knowledge troubled me. "We heard you were with Prince Rupert."

Before he replied Roderick Moore glanced around the table and his eyes locked with mine for a long moment.

"We swept the Parliamentary cavalry from the field," he said, stating the fact calmly and not asking for praise. "To my mind His Highness had us ride too far in their pursuit — although I should not criticise my commanding officer! We found the King's foot-soldiers in some need when we returned."

I did not like the way Edmund curled his lip and wondered why he was not in accord with our visitor. Surely, I thought with a stab of anxiety, my own interest in Mr Moore was not so very evident? I had taken pains to mask it. Could it be that Edmund Haughton was envious of the more flamboyant figure cut by our guest?

It was difficult for me to form coherent thought at all. The one thing I was really sure of that evening was a singing inward gladness that Roderick Moore was *alive*. Everything else paled into insignificance!

I was in Sorrel's stall next morning, making a pretence of grooming her but in reality keeping an anxious ear cocked for Mr Moore's departure. When he came to the stables he walked straight across to the stall and looked at me over the half-door.

"Good!" he said, with undisguised satisfaction. "I had hoped to find you here, Mistress Beth!"

"G-good morning, sir!" I stammered

feebly. "I — I came to see to Sorrel. She is a trifle lame, I fear."

He leaned over the door, a lazy smile upon his handsome face and my heart gave a ridiculous flutter. In the pale, cold light of the December morning, he seemed even taller and darker than usual.

"Poor Sorrel!" he said, his voice expressing disbelief at her lameness — which was of course a fabrication on my part.

I was not about to admit having waited for him! He stroked the mare's questing nose and quirked a dark brow at me.

"Last night," he said, "you gazed on me as if I were a ghost, new-risen, and you were so lacking in colour I thought you faint. You did not expect to see me again, did you, Beth? Yet — why? I said it would be so!"

I looked away and rested my hand upon Sorrel's smooth side for support.

"I — I thought you dead, sir," I whispered hesitantly. Then, accusingly,

I stared at him and said: "You are not dead, so you must have been merely wounded! Was the wound bad, sir?"

Roderick Moore narrowed those dark blue eyes of his and frowned at me.

"Wound? Who spoke of my being wounded?" he said softly. "I vow *I* have said nothing of it."

My hand moved swiftly to give a light tap at his right shoulder and I heard his breath hiss in a wince of pain.

"Oh — forgive me, sir!" I gasped, aghast at my action. "That was extremely thoughtless of me."

He stared at me frowningly.

"How came you by this knowledge, Beth Gaunt?" he asked in puzzlement. "You knew even the location of the wound." He gave a sudden boyish grin, then added: "I have it — witchcraft!"

I started violently and backed from his teasing gaze, colliding with Sorrel as I moved.

"You must not say that, sir!" I said through dry lips. "Even in jest, you *must* not say it!" He was eyeing me oddly, as well he might. I tried to smile and failed miserably, knowing I must offer some form of rational explanation. "I — I had a dream," I said draggingly. "There was a battle and you were there and you were struck. You fell and I thought you were dead." I bit my lip and said: "It was only a dream! Pray do not stare at me like that! It was *not* witchcraft!"

I waited anxiously for his reaction. Over the gap of the years I seemed to hear my mother's voice, begging that I keep my strange power a secret. Roderick Moore was very still and I clenched my hands, waiting for him to speak.

"You dreamed of me, Beth?" he said at last. "That means you did not forget me when I rode away."

The expression in his eyes warned me I was facing a new danger, every bit as potent as the accusation of witchcraft. I rushed into speech before Roderick laid bare his thoughts.

"Of course I did not forget you, sir," I said lightly enough. "I thought of you sometimes — as I thought of Mr Haughton and Edmund. I thought of all of you, facing the dangers of war. Surely it was natural that I should do so?"

He beckoned me out into the stableyard and I left the comforting warmth of Sorrel and faced him in the damp, cold air.

"Do not shy away from me, Beth," he said, that warm expression in his eyes still. "Sometimes I feel you are but a child. On other occasions — " he paused. "Your position here is uncertain. Do not contradict, Beth — of *course* it is uncertain. What of your future? Can it be that you are betrothed to Edmund Haughton? It would explain much."

My eyes went wide and I felt my colour rise. Perhaps I should not have revealed even that I had dreamed of him! He thought I favoured him and was fighting my emotions on account of being betrothed to Edmund! Thoroughly disconcerted, I found I could only stare at him.

"You puzzle me, Beth," he went on, his tone lighter. "Sometimes I feel I have always known you. On other occasions we are strangers to each other." He sighed and touched me fleetingly upon the cheek with a gentle finger. "Whatever we may be to each other, I am sure it is not meant that we should be enemies."

"Enemies?" I echoed uncomfortably. "You and I — enemies? Of course, we are not, sir!"

He eyed me unsmilingly.

"If there is no betrothal between you and Edmund Haughton your position here is not secure, think what you may, Beth Gaunt! Remember well what I said to you. There could come a time when you need sanctuary. My mother would be happy to take you in and I am sure that you would like Moorend."

I moved restlessly from his gaze.

"I love Brackenthorpe," I said doggedly. "I would never leave here willingly. I would do anything to stay here for ever!"

"Anything?" he asked, raising a dark brow. "Can nothing ever compete with your love for a mere *house*? Beth — you trouble me! I would prefer to think you eager to remain here for young Haughton's sake, rather than judge you obsessed with Brackenthorpe Hall! Ah," he said, when I made no attempt to respond, "I had best be on my way. You are a child still, Beth Gaunt — I was foolish to think you otherwise."

I bit my lip, unsure of his meaning, unsure of anything — even for this moment of my avowed intent to cling to Brackenthorpe.

"I — I am not a child, sir," I protested half-heartedly. "Soon I will be seventeen."

"To me seventeen sounds remarkably young," said Roderick Moore half mockingly. "I am four and twenty."

"Oh," I murmured helplessly.

The conversation seemed to be leading nowhere at all but still I did not wish him to go. I felt a sense of impending loss. Our short time together had been wasted with meaningless words. For a brief, breathless moment I considered agreeing to travel north to his home. Would even leaving Brackenthorpe be worse than parting in this less than amicable way? In the next breath I was reproaching myself bitterly. Mr Moore was right! I was so childishly uncertain of myself!

Little more passed between us and when he was gone I sought the comfort of Sorrel and wept a little against her smooth neck. My thoughts were all with the departed royalist and when a voice spoke quietly behind me I started guiltily and spun round.

"Edmund!" I murmured unwelcomingly.

"What ails you, Beth?" he asked me stiffly. "You are weeping. Can it be that you mourn Roderick Moore's departure? He is nothing to you. You may never see him again!"

"Weeping? For Mr Moore?" I said in the lightest tone I could muster. "Of course I do not weep for him!" I rushed on: "I think his presence made me think too deeply on this horrid war — where men must die and — "

Edmund eyed me unsmilingly.

"Come, Beth," he urged me impatiently. "You were weeping for Moore. Why deny it?"

I hesitated, then gave a reluctant nod.

"He was wounded in the battle," I muttered. "He could so easily have been killed — and so could you, Edmund. I hate this war already and your father says it is far from over!"

"Poor Beth!" said Edmund wryly. He put an arm about my shoulders. "Come back into the house, love. You are half-frozen. I suppose you have been waiting about in the cold for an hour or more — just to bid him farewell?" When I hung my head

Edmund shrugged. "I shall not scold you, Beth, for liking Moore! He is a good-looking fellow and attractive to the ladies." I glanced up, half-annoyed by his possessively forgiving tone. "Beth," he went on, "you said once that you felt you *belonged* here at Brackenthorpe. Would you marry me — if that should prove possible? I know I do not cut a romantic figure in the manner of Roderick Moore but you liked me well enough before this war began."

I sighed and interrupted him.

"Perhaps I am still too young to know my own mind, Edmund," I murmured, striving to be honest with him. "You know that, even if we were both sure of our feelings, there would be strenuous opposition from your family. We would need great determination to go against your parents' wishes."

He capitulated with unflattering eagerness.

"Yes — I suppose you are right, Beth!" he agreed. "We will leave matters as they stand for now. There is no hurry to make a decision — now I know you do not mourn Moore's going to the exclusion of all else."

His expression lightened and he kissed my cheek, took my hand and led me into the house at his side. When I was alone I endeavoured to bring order to my own emotions. What was amiss with me? How could it be that I should feel the beginnings of love for both Edmund and Roderick Moore? With Edmund my future would be settled. He would have me as his wife — if he dared to defy his family. Roderick had offered me infinitely less! Why must I hesitate between the two of them? With Edmund I would also gain my beloved Brackenthorpe. I had no choice but to forget Roderick Moore. As Edmund had said, it was likely I would never again *see* my royalist friend!

Edmund was right, I thought unhappily. Roderick had been a romantic figure who appealed to my fickle nature. It was high time that I left the realms of childish fantasy and dwelled upon the solid fact that Edmund Haughton had declared a wish to marry me. It would have been easier, I pondered ruefully, if Edmund had not guessed I had any feeling for Roderick. When I learned that Elizabeth too had witnessed that parting in the stableyard I wished that I had never ventured out of doors that morning.

"Bessie Gaunt — the blacksmith's brat!" taunted Elizabeth. "First you try to bewitch my brother and now you must have Mr Moore also! Are you never satisfied? It is not as if you are even well-looking or — or talented," she went on, her grievance developing. "Why should you expect the gentlemen to take heed of you? You do not even *belong* here! You are just on my father's charity!"

The younger girl was actually jealous of me, I marvelled. She, who had everything — a loving family and a share in Brackenthorpe, envied *me*! Though she was but fourteen, it seemed that she had succumbed to the charm of our royalist visitor. I had learned to accept her hatred. Her *jealousy* was something new. I was unused to being the object of envy.

My five years at Brackenthorpe had taught me how materially poor had been my childhood. Elizabeth had taken for granted the luxury of her life and her home. Perhaps she had also taken for granted the fact that a visiting gentleman would favour her, as daughter of the house, against all others. Poor Elizabeth, I thought wryly. She, who had never known need and had despised my background, was now admitting to feeling inferior. Had mine been a truly noble nature I might have told her there and then that she need not fear competition from me in her hope for Mr Moore's approval. My path *must* lie with Edmund and Brackenthorpe!

Instead of setting Elizabeth's mind at rest I was guilty of enjoying her discomfiture. Had she been kinder to me in the past I would have answered her differently.

"I cannot help it if I am admired, Elizabeth!" I told her. "I do indeed hope I have the friendship of both Edmund and Mr Moore!"

Christmas was a very quiet occasion this year. We did all the usual things but somehow the spirit of gaiety was lacking. This war, which tore our country in two, was at the back of all of our minds and spoiled all hope of enjoyment. Edmund must have had further thoughts of opposing his parents' wishes on the subject of marrying me for he embraced me beneath the kissing-bunch before their very eyes, his manner defiant rather than loving. Mr Haughton smiled a shade stiffly and said how fortunate Edmund was — having two pretty *sisters* to tease! From the looks exchanged by father and son I realised that I must have been discussed and that Edmund had been reprimanded. His behaviour now was evidently intended as a sign that he would go his own way in spite of his parents. I was unsure whether to be pleased or otherwise by Edmund's new firm manner. Soon he would be of age and would not need to consider wishes other than his own. The thought disturbed me. With a slight sinking of my heart I acknowledged the fact that my rosy plans for the future concerned Edmund himself less than they concerned Brackenthorpe. Guiltily, I suppressed the memory of Roderick Moore's words: *"Can nothing compete with your love for a mere house?"*

Several weeks after Christmas we heard that there had been a royalist victory in distant Cornwall. A gentleman called Sir Ralph Hopton had defeated a parliamentary army there. This news made our gentlemen increasingly restless and I knew it would not be long before they left us again. Mistress Haughton made loud protest when they announced their intention of riding south to rejoin the King.

"I am sure the war has gone on well enough without you!" she said tartly.

"Cecilia," said her husband wearily. "Let us have an end to this! My place, and Edmund's also, is with the King. This news of a success in Cornwall is cheering in the extreme and we have dallied here quite long enough. We have a part to play. You must play yours, here at home!"

His tone was mild but firm and his wife did not attempt to argue further. Indeed I could see she was angry with herself for displaying her feelings so openly in my presence. I fiddled with my needlework and affected disinterest.

Mr Haughton and Edmund rode south with the northern army beneath the banner of the Earl of Newcastle although their intention was to join the King's own army in Oxford. Apparently His Majesty had made this town his headquarters. He had gone there at about the time when the Haughtons arrived home. We had no word of where

Prince Rupert's army was now situated so I could not judge where Roderick Moore might be at this moment.

It was useless to condemn my interest in Mr Moore. Even though I had decided I must marry Edmund I could not forget this royalist who fought beneath the banner of the Prince from Germany. Well — my thoughts were my own and if I chose to think of Roderick sometimes that was entirely my affair!

A letter arrived during the summer of 1643. It was brought by one of Mr Haughton's servants who had been injured, he said, in a "skirmish with Roundheads" and had been sent home to recuperate. The servant was Dick Short and he was little more than a boy. The meaning of war was emphasised horridly to us all when poor young Dick died of his wound within a week of his return. Mistress Haughton tended him to the last personally and I found myself unwillingly admiring her when she announced his death with the suspicion of a tear in her normally hard eyes.

That letter, brought by the unfortunate Dick, revealed very little except perhaps a greater need for secrecy. Surely Mr Haughton did not think we harboured spies of Parliament at Brackenthorpe!

Mistress Haughton, in a softened frame of mind following Dick's death, read out the letter when I was present.

"The plan to encircle London and thus take the capital for the King has failed," she read. "We verge upon another meeting but more than this is not safe to say. Sometimes we feel the enemy is pre-warned of all our plans. In writing letters to our homes we may be endangering our cause. I am trusting Dick Short to guard this well."

Poor Dick had guarded it all too well, I thought soberly. If he had broken his journey to have his wound properly tended he might have saved his young life.

It sounded extremely likely that another great battle of the like of

Edgehill was envisaged in the near future. I tried not to think of the thousands of luckless men who might not survive. How this whole, sorry affair would end was beyond my puny reasoning. I was powerless to do anything save pray for those I loved.

6

MISTRESS HAUGHTON'S softer mood suffered quick alteration once Dick Short's sad funeral was over. On the morning of the next day she summoned me to her side for what proved to be a most illuminating interview.

"Bessie," she began in a harsh though guarded tone, "there is something I must say to you. I had hoped never to speak on this subject — a painful one to me. However, matters have gone quite far enough. My son's foolish infatuation for you leads me to deal with you straightly. This must be resolved before he next comes home. Either you are ignorant of the situation or fully aware and using it against me."

She paused and I looked at her uncertainly.

"I will not leave Brackenthorpe — unless

Mr Haughton bids me go," I said hurriedly. "He chose to bring me here and only he could make me leave. Elizabeth has always said that you will rid yourself of me in your husband's absence. Well — I will not go! If Edmund loves me, then why cannot we be wed?"

Having brought the matter thus into the open, I clasped my hands tightly behind my back and stared at Edmund's mother with half-fearful defiance.

"You will never wed my son, Bessie Gaunt," she said, pursing her lips. "It appears that you do know nothing, after all! My husband kept the truth from you."

"I have not the slightest idea what you mean, ma'am," I told her, wary of the argument she was to use to separate me from Edmund but in total ignorance of her meaning.

"You cannot wed Edmund," she said, watching me carefully. "It would be sinful! You see, Bessie, I have known from the start the reason for your being foisted upon us. Despite my own inclination I have done my duty towards you."

I stared at her for a long moment, then realisation dawned. Her belief was so ludicrous that I felt half-inclined to laugh.

"Mistress Haughton," I managed unsteadily, "have you thought, for all of these years, that your husband is my *father*? Is this the reason why you have tolerated my presence at Brackenthorpe?"

"He has a responsibilty towards you," she said stiffly, a spot of colour high in each cheek. "I had no option but to take you in and to deal fairly with you. It has not been easy, Bessie Gaunt!" With an angry frown, she added: "This talk is most unseemly. It was necessary, though, to point out the total impossibility of marriage between you and Edmund. Even now," she went on, "I am not completely convinced that you have not known this all along."

"You misjudge me, ma'am," I said quietly, "as do you misjudge the situation. My father was Daniel Gaunt. Before that day when he came to our village I had never set eyes upon your husband. I can remember my father's looks plainly, ma'am. I favour him strongly — as I do *not* favour Mr Haughton." I drew in a quivering breath. "My father died at your husband's hand, Mistress Haughton. Although it was an accident your husband felt in my debt and offered me a home." Her hard eyes were still disbelieving. Curiously I said to her: "You must never have asked Mr Haughton for the truth. How you must have tormented yourself, ma'am, all of these years. You have even thought I pretended a wish to wed Edmund, merely to upset you. You do not know me at all. I am sorry for you, ma'am!"

She drew herself up haughtily,

"Have the goodness not to pity me, Bessie Gaunt!" she ordered acidly and left the room.

The matter was never again spoken of directly but Mistress Haughton must have believed what I told her for her treatment of me altered. She was no longer unwillingly tolerant and I was in no doubt that my position in the household had altered. She seemed now to enjoy giving me the bitter lash of her tongue — on those occasions when she did not ignore me completely.

The kitchen-maid left without warning, further depleting Brackenthorpe's staff of servants. I knew that Mistress Haughton would have dearly loved to have relegated *me* to the kitchen in the girl's stead. Something — possibly fear of her husband's displeasure — made her refrain from so drastic a step but she did oblige me to take on kitchen duties occasionally, coolly saying that straitened times were upon us.

For the running of this large establishment there were now far fewer servants than was necessary. Old Jacob, William, Cook and a middle-aged maid by the name of Kate were all that remained of the formerly large staff. I supposed wryly that it was only to be expected that my tasks should double themselves in number now I had denied all relationship with the family.

It became speedily obvious that, try as we might, Brackenthorpe Hall and its grounds could not be kept up to accustomed standard. Discounting the grounds, the house itself contained too many rooms for us to keep in reasonable order.

Without consulting anyone else, Mistress Haughton put in action a plan for cutting down the necessary amount of toil. She assembled the four servants, Elizabeth and myself in the hall and made known to us her decision.

"I am going to close off the upper part of the east wing," she said. "Elizabeth and Bessie must move over into bedchambers in the west wing, close to mine. Cook and Kate may continue in their rooms beside the kitchen, as the kitchen-floor will not be affected. It is not sensible to keep open that whole upper floor. Apart from Elizabeth and Bessie's rooms there are only guest-rooms and guests are highly unlikely at this time. Once Jacob and William have put out dust-covers we will leave the east wing untouched — until my husband returns with the other servants."

I had to admit the sense of this plan. However the gleam in Mistress Haughton's eyes when she looked at me warned that more than the closing of the wing was involved. Elizabeth and I moved our personal belongings from our rooms and took them across the gallery and into the west wing. Elizabeth's new chamber opened from her mother's and was large and well appointed, as befitted the daughter of the house.

"Bessie — you will do well enough in here," said the mistress blandly. She ushered me into a tiny room, meagrely furnished with just a narrow servant's bed. There was no chest for my modest wardrobe of gowns, just two hooks in the wall beside the door. "You will be cosy in here," said Mistress Haughton with a grim smile.

The satisfaction on her face made me wonder if this move had been made more to spite me than to lessen the number of rooms to be cleaned. With a fair attempt at a smile I said I would do very well in here — once Jacob and William had brought my clothes chest over from the east wing. Her eyes locked with mine for a long moment, then she shrugged indifferently and gave the order to the menservants. My victory was small and afforded little satisfaction. True, I now had somewhere to put my gowns but very little space was left between the heavy chest and that narrow bed.

I wondered what Mr Haughton would make of the new arrangements. No doubt his wife would tell him this slip of a room was my own choice. With a heavy sigh I set out my pewter-ware and my bible upon the chest. They looked well enough but I would have to lift them off when I wished to open the chest.

Stepping back to view my prized possessions in their new setting, I collided painfully with the open door of my cramped quarters. Sinking down upon the bed, my spirits low, I rubbed my bruised elbow. Then I rose to my feet and squared my shoulders. I would not let Mistress Haughton defeat me! I would make the best of this small room.

Thoughtfully I gazed around. With the chest alongside the bed and beneath the tall, narrow window, only a small space existed. If the chest would fit between the head of the bed and the window-wall a much larger space would be available! I put my bible and pewter-ware on the bed and heaved at the chest with all my strength. I was breathless and panting by the time I had it in its desired place. Enthusiasm firing me, I made several trips back across the gallery to my old room.

The result of all my efforts pleased me. Although the room was small it now wore a comfortable, friendly air. My pewter-ware was on the window-ledge. My bible was on the chest beside my bed. My washing-bowl was at the other end of the chest. A rag rug covered the small floor-space and a stool was beneath the window. The elegant bedcoverlet from my old room, though too large and folded in half, transformed the narrow bed.

I stood in the open doorway and gave a smile of satisfaction. Mistress Haughton's spite was of no avail! I actually *liked* my new bedchamber!

Elizabeth grumbled endlessly at the move and earned her mother's displeasure when she continued to cross the gallery for items from her old room.

"This plan will fail in its object, Elizabeth," said the mistress sharply, "if you intend to trail from one wing to the other in this foolish fashion! Must I lock the gallery door? Remember, Elizabeth — and you, too, Bessie Gaunt — in Mr Haughton's absence I am in sole charge here. There will be no more grumbling from either of you!" she ended.

"I do not grumble, ma'am," I reminded her. "I have not complained at my lot, have I?"

She gave an impatient sniff and left us.

"Does Mother know how much *you* have brought over from your old room, Bessie?" asked Elizabeth spitefully. "She'd be annoyed if she saw how comfortable you've made it."

"I have not given you leave to pry in my room, Elizabeth," I reminded her, then smiled, always eager to improve our relationship. "Come — shall I help you to set out your new chamber in a manner more to your liking?"

Elizabeth glared.

"Don't you *dare* to patronise me, Bessie Gaunt!" she cried. "Father brought you out of your poverty and improved your status and you think you are better than any of us — so do not deny it! I hate you!"

With a sigh I left her. It seemed we could never be friends — Elizabeth Haughton and I. She vowed she hated me, yet I had done nothing to earn her hatred. Now, it seemed, she even envied me of the improvements I had made to my poor little bed-chamber! When I encountered her mother, minutes later, I was reprimanded for being unkind to the younger girl.

"Elizabeth is most upset at your treatment of her, Bessie Gaunt," Mistress Haughton informed me coldly. "I had thought one in your position would set aside airs and graces and be more helpful in these troubled times. You have much to be grateful for, Bessie, yet you have an odd way of showing your gratitude."

"Your daughter's opinion of me falls in line with your own, mistress," I said wearily. "Neither of you like me in the least! You know full well that

I have tried to be friendly towards Elizabeth. She takes her cue from you and treats me accordingly. I have done nothing to earn the dislike of either of you."

Mistress Haughton's eyes narrowed. "Nothing?" she grated. "You can say you have done *nothing*! You, the blacksmith's brat, wormed yourself into my husband's affections and into our home. Now, as if by witchcraft, you turn your wiles upon my son! Mark me well, Bessie Gaunt — if you succeed in marrying Edmund, it will be across my dead body!"

I shivered, a chill in my heart. That word "witchcraft" robbed me of the power to retaliate — to answer her even. Elizabeth, who had listened from the background, stepped forward now and said in gloating tones:

"See, Mother, how she flinches! She went white as a sheet when you spoke of witchcraft!"

They both eyed me closely and I shivered anew.

"There is something odd about you, Bessie," pondered Mistress Haughton. She exchanged a glance with Elizabeth. "Only a witch could hold our gentlemen's affections against their will," she said, reaching for my shoulder with spiteful fingers.

Elizabeth added eagerly:

"Remember that time in the still-room, Mother! Bessie acted in a strange fashion, did she not? She spoke of a battle even before we learned that one had taken place. Witchcraft?" She rolled the word about her tongue. "It would explain so much!"

I wriggled out of Mistress Haughton's hurtful clutch, appalled by the turn of the conversation.

"You are both crazed!" I choked. "You know I am no witch! You would be afraid of my power if you truly believed your own words. Witches are supposed to perform evil deeds. All *I* wish is to be left in peace to live here at Brackenthorpe!"

With this I fled outside to the

stable-yard, my heart thumping in the region of my throat until it threatened to suffocate me. For the next few days Elizabeth plagued and taunted me with both veiled and direct remarks about witchcraft. I knew she did not believe anything of her accusations but I was set in utmost fear. Looking closely into my own nature and what had gone before, I had my own doubts — made no easier by her heartless teasing. Could it be that I was in fact a witch? What would I do if anything should happen which gave more credence to the jibes of the Haughton ladies? My last waking thoughts each night were of the swimming of the witch I had witnessed so very long ago.

One hot summer day in the month of August matters came sharply to a head. I had been working in the herb-garden and, finding the sun's ray's too powerful for my unprotected head, came indoors in search of a bonnet.

I blinked my sun-dazed eyes as I

entered the hall and both Mistress Haughton and Elizabeth turned to stare at me from the seats where they had been taking their ease.

"Finished the weeding already, Bessie?" demanded the mistress, rising to her feet. "We must give you another task, for the Devil finds use for empty hands!"

My head ached from my toil in the sunshine and I pressed an earthy hand to my brow, only to find that the pain had intensified. I gave a moan and swayed on my feet. Dimly I was aware that Elizabeth and her mother were approaching me.

"No — ah, no!" I gasped, as that familiar drumming sounded in my ears.

My protests were in vain for the Dream was upon me. A vision took shape, unasked, before my glazed eyes and I cowered back from it.

"Fire!" I choked, wincing from its imagined but no less fierce heat. "Brackenthorpe is burning! Put out the flames!" My hands covered my eyes in an attempt to shut out the terrifying sight. "Oh — I cannot bear to see Brackenthorpe burn!"

My shoulders were taken in a merciless grip and Mistress Haughton shook me until the Dream departed and I begged for release.

"Bessie is going to burn the house down, Mother!" gasped Elizabeth. "She *must* be a witch!"

"I love this house," I muttered huskily as I shrugged off Mistress Haughton's hands. "I love it above all things but," my voice cracked and tears fell unheeded down my cheeks, "it will burn and be no more. Nothing can alter what must be!"

Elizabeth cringed from me but her mother gave a harsh laugh.

"Very prettily acted, Bessie!" she applauded me. "So you have decided to play along with our taunt of witchcraft, have you? Well, girl, you will not deceive me with your play-acting and dire predictions! Would you have us think you truly a witch and fear you? When I see Brackenthorpe burn — *then* I may believe you. Until that time, Bessie Gaunt — get back to your work!"

Elizabeth's fears receded in face of her mother's scorn and she laughed when I rushed out headlong through the door, weeping still for what I knew must come.

I could scarcely tell herbs from weeds that day, so blinded by my tears was I, when I returned to the garden.

Had the Dream predicted a true image? Could I hope for less than the burning of my beloved Brackenthorpe? When I had seen Roderick Moore killed in battle he had later proved to be merely injured. Could this horror of burning be a like case? Yet in my vision those consuming flames had eaten hungrily at the very fabric of the house. Nothing could withstand so fierce a blaze!

My dread for Brackenthorpe's future blotted out even my relief that Mistress

Haughton had dismissed the Dream as mere play-acting. If my lovely Brackenthorpe should burn and be no more, then life would be empty indeed.

7

I WAS still at work in the herb-garden, when William came running into view. He was wide-eyed with apprehension.

"Mistress!" he gasped.

"What is amiss, William?" I asked him urgently.

He gulped then cast a hunted look behind him.

"Soldiers, mistress!" he stammered. "Dozens of 'em. They're making for t'house — "

"What kind of soldiers, William?" I interrupted swiftly. "Are they King's men or for Parliament?"

"I — I know not, mistress," admitted William. "Just *soldiers*, they are, wi' orange bands about 'em. What will they do to us? What do they want?"

"Orange sashes?" I said unsteadily. "Then they are Roundheads! I doubt if

133

they will be kindly intentioned towards this — a royalist home!"

I lifted my skirts and fled into the house through the kitchen entrance. I was panting for breath when I found Mistress Haughton and Elizabeth in the hall. The mistress eyed me disapprovingly.

"Bessie Gaunt — look at your shoes, girl! They are covered in mud and you are trampling it all over the floor — "

"Roundheads, ma'am!" I burst in shakily. "William saw them. They are coming up to the house. They must be almost at the door! What must we do?"

Elizabeth gave a shriek of terror.

"Oh — they will kill us all!" she moaned.

Mistress Haughton gripped her daughter's arm and dragged her towards the stairs.

"Greet the soldiers, Bessie," she cried to me across her shoulder. "Keep them talking and give us time to hide our jewellery. My husband warned me of this possibility. They will strip the house of all that is valuable and depart with their plunder! It has happened already to homes in the south."

Mother and daughter fled up the broad stairway, Elizabeth stumbling and sobbing all the while. They left me standing there in the hall, with my muddy shoes, my earthy hands and my trembling knees. Hearing raised voices and the clatter of feet as the main door opened, I fought down my panic, hid my hands behind my back and faced Jacob as he hobbled up to me. The old man was in a state of near-collapse.

"Mistress — there's a captain come wi' his soldiers," he began in quavering tones.

He was stating the obvious. The parliamentary captain and at least six of his men had not waited to be announced. They were already in the hall behind Jacob. They wore buff-coats, breastplates, steel helmets and extremely grim expressions. Their swords and pistols were much in evidence and I felt my ankles buckling. I stiffened my back when old Jacob subsided on to the nearest stool, lifted my chin and faced the leader of the intruders. He was short-statured, not much taller than I was and his weather-beaten face was like that of a farmer. On sight of me he had removed his helmet, so he must have held some pretension to gentility.

"Captain Braddock, ma'am," he greeted me with stiff civility. I inclined my head but said nothing, waiting for him to state his intentions. "This is Brackenthorpe Hall — home of one Laurence Haughton?" he went on harshly. Still I nodded dumbly. "Mistress Haughton — you are about to help us."

I found my voice at last but did not contradict his assumption of my identity.

"Help you, sir?" I murmured through dry lips. "We are all women here at Brackenthorpe except for Jacob here and one slow-witted boy. I very much doubt that it is in our power to help you."

Braddock's eyes had been scanning the hall as I spoke. Bringing them back again to me, he frowned.

"We know of your unprotected state, mistress," he said shortly. "We do not intend to harm you." Staring round at those silent, armed men, I shuddered, finding it difficult to believe him. "We are in need of merely food and horses," he told me. "My men have marched for many days and are hungry. We need horses for our cause."

Suddenly I lifted my chin. He was not even trying to word a *request*. He knew this was a royalist household and was demanding that which we were not willing to give.

"And if we refuse, sir?" I asked, wishing all the while that Mistress Haughton would appear and order the soldiers from her home.

Captain Braddock gave a harsh, humourless chuckle.

"Refusal will avail you naught,

mistress," he told me curtly, gesturing to his men to spread about the house. "My soldiers are already at your stables."

I winced, picturing my poor Sorrel being obliged to take the weight of an armed man. Seeing three soldiers clattering up the stairway, I set aside my thoughts of the horses.

"Captain Braddock!" I said sharply, pointing to the men. "Where are *they* going? They will find neither food not horses up there! Is it really necessary for you to intrude so far upon our privacy? We cannot prevent your — er — *appropriation* of *food* and suchlike — "

I broke off when a scream came from the kitchens. Cook was a hardy enough woman but poor Kate must be terrified out of her wits as she watched the soldiers ransacking the food-store.

The captain gestured to a soldier to investigate the happenings in the kitchen, then turned to me.

"You should be pleased of this

chance to aid your own countrymen against the despot Stuart," he observed crushingly. "Never fear, mistress, we will take only what is needed. You have no necessity in judging this theft. You will be recompensed later. I will leave you my note to this effect."

He was impatient with my doubts and fears and I eyed him with the utmost dislike. Even so, he did not have my full attention. My ears were straining for some sound above stairs to indicate that Mistress Haughton and Elizabeth had been discovered. I hoped the jewellery had been deposited in a safe hiding-place. Old Jacob was sitting on his stool still, whimpering in the manner of an injured animal and I went over to put my hand upon his shoulder.

Captain Braddock had moved off to confer with one of his men and so I sank down on a stool beside Jacob's, praying that the soldiers would leave us soon yet dreading to dwell on the state in which they would leave my lovely Brackenthorpe.

"Where be Mistress Haughton?" muttered Jacob, lifting faded, frightened eyes to mine. "She should stop 'em doing this. 'Tisn't right! Master will be angry wi'us all."

"This is war, Jacob," I told him compassionately. "Do not be fearful. Mr Haughton would not expect you to defend his home singlehanded. We are all powerless against armed soldiers."

I fell silent, knowing that the old man was not heeding my words. I stared round the hall at the hatefully busy soldiers. Captain Braddock had the cropped hair that had given rise to the parliamentarians' nickname but several of the soldiers had longer locks which showed below their steel helmets. Many of them were mere boys, I thought, but they all had the same hard, determined look. To me they seemed true fighting men. I found it hard to picture the gentle Laurence Haughton and his son, riding to battle in their gay plumed hats — against such men as these. My heart had been heavy before but now it took on this additional weight of anxiety. The Haughton gentlemen were dear to me!

I shuffled restlessly upon my hard stool, wondering why the mistress and Elizabeth had not yet appeared. Could it be that they had concealed themselves in some form of hiding-place and had left me to deal with the Roundheads alone? I watched some of the soldiers carrying food from the kitchen. A lavish spread began to appear upon that long table where I took my meals with the family. I saw that some of the food was being parcelled up and taken outside but it was evident that the uninvited guests intended to dine here before they left us.

"There'll be naught left for any of *us*, mistress," muttered Jacob in anguish. "I should stop 'em, shouldn't I? I should tell 'em all to go!"

"You can do nothing, Jacob," I reassured him. "Oh, why does Mistress

Haughton not come down? Surely she cannot be hiding till the soldiers leave? It would be unworthy of her!"

I rose abruptly to my feet, squared my shoulders and moved to stand beside the table. Finding Captain Braddock's eyes upon me, I said bitterly:

"Must your men take all the food in the house, sir? What is to become of us when you are gone?"

A frown creased his brow as he opened his mouth to answer me. However, just at that moment, there came a shout from the kitchen.

"*Fire!*"

Kate ran screaming into the hall, a dripping ladle in her hand, and I saw smoke pouring out through the kitchen door. There were shouts of both fear and consternation and the soldiers nearest to the kitchen began to cough with the smoke. I was never sure of the sequence of events after this for, to my everlasting shame, I fell into a deep swoon. My Dream of fire had become reality. Brackenthorpe was burning!

When I came to my senses I was no longer in the hall. I found I was sitting on the stone steps of the front entrance of the house, old Jacob beside me, and a young buff-coated soldier seeming to be standing guard over us. The soldier was little more than a boy and he gave a gulp of relief when I opened my eyes and rose unsteadily to my feet.

"Eh — you had me worried there, mistress!" he said with rough concern. "Captain Braddock said as how he'd hold me responsible for your safety. I thought as you'd gone an' died on me!"

"It was stupid of me to swoon," I said slowly. "I am quite well now." I gazed around uncomprehendingly. "The house is still standing. I — I expected to see it burned to the ground."

The young soldier gaped at me.

"There's no damage done, save to the kitchens and what lies over 'em, mistress," he told me. "The hall and gallery and that other wing are untouched. Captain Braddock soon had everything under control."

"Was anyone injured?" I said next, as I peered into the hall which was still full of smoke.

"Aye," nodded the soldier. "Trooper Bell had his arms burned and some of the others were overcome by smoke." He hesitated and nodded to Jacob, who was staring blankly into space. "I reckon this 'un is badly shocked. Your cook went wild at the men! I reckon she's still in there, lashing 'em wi' her tongue!"

The smoke was beginning to clear in the hall now but everywhere seemed very wet and an unpleasant, acrid smell hung in the air. My legs were strangely stiff and moving them at all was something of an effort. When I saw Mistress Haughton being carried down the broad stairway by two burly soldiers, my knees buckled beneath me and I clutched at the door-frame. Old

Jacob stumbled past me and gazed in horror at the limp figure of his mistress.

"You've killed her, you murdering Roundheads!" he cried. "You've killed Mistress Haughton!"

He lapsed into sobbing silence when the soldier nearest to him delivered a cuff in his direction. The blow was merely a glancing one but the old servant staggered on his feet. I moved forwards unsteadily, crying out:

"Leave him alone, you great lout! Why — he is half out of his mind and old enough to be your grandfather!"

I pushed my way through the suddenly silent soldiers and approached the foot of the stairs. I stared down at Mistress Haughton as she lay unconscious on the floor where the men had deposited her. Captain Braddock appeared at my side. He listened gravely to what the men told him, then bent swiftly over the mistress. Slowly he rose to his feet and turned to me.

"She is not dead," he said. "My soldiers found her raving to herself upstairs. They say she was quite demented. These keys," he handed them to me, "were clutched in her hand. When my men approached her she crumpled before them and lost consciousness. I would advise that she is taken up to her bed."

He ordered the shivering, weeping Kate to accompany the soldiers who lifted up her mistress once more. I gazed for a long moment as they ascended the stairs. Then, drawn by some force stronger than my own will, I walked past the captain, crossed the hall and came to a halt at the open door to the kitchen quarters.

Everything appeared to be completely burnt out and the heavy, choking smell of smoke hung in the air. Water — fetched, presumably, from the well or the stream — lay several inches deep upon the floor and I could see the charred remains of the kitchen table, where the servants took their meals. I had not realised until now that a kind of numbness had me in its grip. When I raised my eyes to what had been the kitchen ceiling my veil of apathy vanished.

The savage fury of the flames had seared upwards, devouring not only the ceiling but also the rooms above — rooms which had belonged until recently to Elizabeth and myself.

Elizabeth!

I took a backward step from the smoking ruin of the kitchen. Where was Elizabeth Haughton? Surely my senses must have been lacking, not to have registered that she was still absent?

Without a word to anyone, I picked up my skirts, wove my way amongst the smoke-grimed soldiers, who had gone stolidly back to the parcelling-up of their plunder, and ascended the stairs in breathless urgency.

Frantically, I searched the rooms of the unharmed west wing, looking beneath beds and behind hangings, calling softly for the missing girl. My search was fruitless. I paused, biting my lip, by the closed door of Mistress Haughton's room, then tapped and entered.

The maid, Kate, was sitting on a stool at the bedside of her unconscious mistress, her cap and apron blackened by smoke. She was muttering to herself and when I spoke her name, she turned blank eyes on me.

"'Twas my fault," she said tonelessly and began to rock rhythmically on her stool. "I started the fire. I never thought 'twould flare up like that. 'Twas too fierce to be put out."

When I tried to question her she fell stubbornly silent and continued that disturbing rocking with her eyes closed. I turned my attention to Mistress Haughton. She lay flat upon her back with the coverlet pulled up to her chin. Her eyes were still closed and, but for the faint movement of the coverlet over her breast, I would have judged her spirit departed. Putting a hand upon her shoulder, I gave her a gentle shake.

"Elizabeth, mistress!" I implored her in a whisper. "Where is Elizabeth? Where is she hiding?"

Cecilia Haughton's eyes fluttered open but they were devoid of all expression. Urgently I repeated my question and was rewarded by seeing her lips move in silent speech.

"Kate," I demanded across the bed at the maid, "has your mistress spoken at all since she was carried up here? What has happened to put her into this state? *Where* is Mistress Elizabeth?"

Kate's only response was a more violent rocking of her bony frame and a muttered moan of despair beneath her breath. Helplessly I looked again at first one woman and then the other. It seemed that neither was to be of help in finding the missing Elizabeth. Biting hard on my lip, I left the bedchamber and made my way to the stairs — only to come to a halt halfway down them.

Captain Braddock was waiting at the foot and by his side was another man. The newcomer was vaguely familiar to me but it was not until he had removed his helmet and spoken that I realised his identity.

"This is indeed an unhappy affair, Mistress Elizabeth," observed Mr Jonas Hardcastle heavily. "I had not thought to find the family of my misguided friend, Laurence Haughton, in such dire straits." When I gaped at him, unable to find words to frame a suitable response and gripping at the banister-rail with one nerveless hand, he went on sympathetically: "You poor child! First there was the unfortunate accident which fired your home and now I hear the ill tidings that your lady mother is struck down with shock."

I stared at him blankly, still at a loss what to say to him. He stood before me, wearing a buff-coat, armour, a sword and an expression of deep regret for what had taken place. He had reached the conclusion that I was

Elizabeth Haughton, daughter of his old acquaintance.

"Captain Hardcastle, the girl is obviously suffering from shock also," put in Captain Braddock, deference masking his impatience at this delay in his plans. "There is little else my men can do here. We are provisioned and have dallied long enough in dealing with the fire."

Jonas Hardcastle looked slowly round at the laden troopers with their purloined goods and I saw a nerve twitch in his cheek. It appeared that he owned rather more of a conscience than did Captain Braddock.

"Go, by all means, Braddock," he said shortly. "I will remain here and do all that is necessary."

I slumped down bonelessly on the stairs and stayed there, gazing almost vacantly as the captain marshalled his men and departed. When all was quiet and no one remained except for poor old Jacob, sitting on that same stool beside the hearth as if chained to it,

Jonas Hardcastle raised me to my feet and brought me down the remaining stairs with solicitous care.

"I cannot say how this has distressed me, mistress," he said heavily. "I beg you will remember that *I* had no part in it! Although your father and I are divided in opinion and loyalty, we remain friends of long standing. Your lady mother is in no case to deal with matters and I am needed elsewhere." He chewed reflectively upon his lip. "I must go but I shall leave two of my men here with you to make safe your ruined wing. Also, I will endeavour to send a doctor to attend poor Mistress Haughton." He spread his hands and stared at me earnestly. "A heavy burden is now upon your young shoulders, Mistress Elizabeth. When your father returns you must tell him how I did my best for you in your time of need."

Mr Haughton's good opinion still mattered to this man I must now call *Captain* Hardcastle, I thought, wearily incredulous. I knew that I should have corrected his error and told him that I was not Elizabeth Haughton — that I was merely Beth Gaunt, whom he had once met and obviously forgotten. However, I held my tongue on this score and let him depart from Brackenthorpe still in ignorance of the truth. Instinct seemed to warn me of the sense of this.

Two strange, strained days went by. The only food in the house was that little left upon the table in the hall by those uniformed marauders. The men left by Captain Hardcastle worked well, if sullenly, in clearing out the charred remains from the kitchen-quarters. They also worked up vast appetites which made something of an inroad upon our meagre rations. Neither Kate nor Mistress Haughton had taken in anything more nourishing than gruel and Cook, Jacob and I ate sparingly from necessity.

The mystery of Elizabeth's disappearance had still not been solved — nor had the vanished William returned. I had searched both the house and the stables without success.

Old Jacob seemed to have retreated permanently into a private silent world of his own making but at least was capable of performing small tasks, once the materials were put into his hands. He worked slowly and without interest on cleaning knives and other utensils but he did *work* — which was more than could be said for Kate, above stairs.

In this dreadful time of shock and disbelief only Cook remained both my friend and my support. I had begun to confide in her Jonas Hardcastle's belief that I was the daughter of the house but she had interrupted me briskly and admitted to eavesdropping on my conversation with the captain. She counselled me to continue to hold my tongue on the truth.

"With t'master away and t'mistress in a state o' living death and Mistress 'Lizabeth missing there's none to lay claim to Brackenthorpe but you, mistress," she pointed out. "If t'Round-heads come back and find none o' t' family here, they'll take over, mark my words, *Mistress Elizabeth*!"

I bit my lip and accepted her advice and the name she so firmly bestowed on me. After all, my name *was* Elizabeth and I would be merely playing a part until Mr Haughton arrived home to take charge.

We had judged the worst to be past but still had something extremely shocking to face. When the two soldiers explored the damaged part of the wing above the kitchens they found the pathetic remains of a young girl. I wept bitterly for poor Elizabeth who must have chosen that fateful spot as her hiding-place when the soldiers arrived. She must have been overcome by smoke and unable to leave the room which had become her tomb. It was then that I recalled being told of Mistress Haughton's collapse. Captain Braddock's men had found her somewhere upstairs — possibly near to the door of the doomed wing — and she had been clutching her bunch of keys. Could it be that she had locked her daughter in for safety, only to learn of the fire in the room below? Small wonder that the mistress was in her present state if my surmise was correct. She would blame herself into eternity for being the cause of Elizabeth's death.

Yes, I wept for the passing of the girl who had refused to be my friend but my tears were shed in secrecy. Cook had identified the body as that of a servant-girl and warned me firmly that I must do nothing to betray the true position.

"This is for the best, mistress," said Cook. "T'poor lass is gone and there's no one to say you're not she. Jacob's gone a-wandering in his wits and that Kate," casting her eyes upwards "is struck near as bad as t'mistress. For t'sake of us as are left — you've got to hold on to Brackenthorpe!"

Weakly I gave in to her arguments and allowed the soldiers to bury poor Elizabeth beneath a tree in Brackenthorpe's grounds. These men had worked well and, although the kitchens and the room above were burnt out and useless, there was now no danger that beams or masonry should fall and maim those of us who remained unharmed.

Their task completed, the soldiers took their leave of us brusquely. It had been all too obvious that they had resented giving aid to a royalist household. The fact that they had complied with Jonas Hardcastle's order could mean that this Roundhead officer was a man of some authority. I was glad he had considered himself a friend of Mr Haughton. But for this we might have fared even worse.

When the soldiers left us William returned. He was haggard and looked half-starved as he led in my mare, Sorrel, and a milk-cow with a rope about its neck. Both of the animals were in good condition — better far than was William himself. Sorrel's soft nose moved questingly about my hair and I felt myself closer to tears than I had been since the finding of Elizabeth's body. William was rightly proud of his cleverness and Cook and I hugged him until he blushed to the roots of his fair hair.

"I thought'twas best to hide Sorrel and t'cow from t'soldiers, mistress," beamed the lad.

I blinked back a tear as I told William he had done well.

"He's a regular hero, Mistress Elizabeth!" said Cook.

William grinned, accepted both our thanks and my new title and said a little plaintively that he was hungry.

Captain Braddock's men had taken the other cow, the two horses belonging to Mistress Haughton and Elizabeth and such of the fowls as they had been able to catch. Three laying-hens had since returned and we had been existing for the past day or so on a meagre diet of eggs and herbs. Now, thanks to William, we could supplement our diet with milk, butter and cheese! Swelling with pride at his own resourcefulness, the lad went on to say that the soldiers had not discovered our store of last year's apples in the loft over the stables and that there were also a few turnip-roots there.

The hearth of the great hall, where once the family had sat at ease, became Cook's new domain. Such was her skill that she was able to produce meals cooked over a low fire there. The soldiers had salvaged some of her pots and utensils and these had been scoured back to their normal state. This task had been performed by old Jacob, who muttered nonsense and grew thinner almost before our eyes. I worried for the old man's health. He, together with the other remaining inhabitants of Brackenthorpe, had become my family and my charge. At last the doctor sent by Captain Hardcastle arrived. After he had shaken his head over

Brackenthorpe's stricken mistress and taken offence when I refused to let him bleed her, I approached him on Jacob's behalf. Stiffly he refused even to look at the old man.

"I have done what I was asked," he said shortly. "More I will not do in this malignant household. I have no duty to those beneath this roof."

He left us with no hope for Mistress Haughton's recovery and no kindly word for any of us. I refused to brood on his attitude and joined Cook in praising William, who had just arrived proudly bearing a rabbit he had snared for the pot. It was evident that no help would be forthcoming from outside sources. We must depend upon our own efforts. No doubt others, suffering at Roundhead hands, would be in worse case than we were. I squared my shoulders and stiffened my resolve. Cook, William and I must shoulder the burden of caring for Brackenthorpe and its invalid occupants. Our resources were slender: we had the minimum of necessities and only the food that we could ourselves provide.

"But," I told myself determinedly and not unhappily, "we have charge of my beloved Brackenthorpe and we have our will to survive. It could be enough! It *shall* be enough!"

8

LYING sleepless on my bed one night in late September, I found myself held fast once more in the grip of the Dream. This time I saw the Haughton gentlemen, clearly recognisable to me in their buff-coats and armour. They were with a small band of similarly clad men and appeared to me to be in the throes of battle. I saw them charge and thrust their swords at the orange-sashed enemy and I saw Edmund receive a slashing blow upon his arm. Edmund was wounded! The scene was so uncomfortably vivid that I almost felt I could hear the hiss of steel, the whinnying of terror-stricken horses and the harsh-drawn breath of these fighting men.

I lay quietly thoughtful when the vision left me and a heavy burden of guilt slowly began to weigh down and oppress me. Edmund Haughton had suffered hurt and yet I felt no urgent desire to weep and wring my hands. Once the Dream had revealed to me that Roderick Moore was injured. *Then* I had near swooned away. Surely it was wrong for me not to show like strong emotion for poor Edmund — he who had declared that he would wed me?

Yet Edmund had not seemed badly hurt, I excused myself swiftly. The vision had not alarmed me unduly because I judged his injury to be slight. Yet, argue as I might, I could not prevent the prick of conscience which insisted I was exhibiting too small a degree of partiality towards Edmund Haughton.

With an exclamation of distress I rolled over to press my face into my pillow. I wept for I knew not what but my chief emotion was one of bitter shame for my own shallow nature.

Several days after this acceptance of unhappy self-revelation we found ourselves giving hospitality to an injured and disillusioned royalist gentleman. He was alone save for one elderly, lame servant and was on his way north to rejoin his family. He had done with war, he informed us bitterly. His injury had occurred at a place called Newbury and three of his oldest and best friends had given up their lives upon that same battlefield. On later reflection I realised that the date he gave us for the battle did not coincide with that of my Dream. Therefore I had to accept that Edmund Haughton's injury must have been received in some place other than Newbury. After so many years of unpleasant familiarity with the Dream I could not find it in myself to doubt its message as other than truth.

Scarcely had the embittered gentleman accepted our food — such as we were able to offer — and our shelter than we were visited by another royalist — this one of my own close acquaintance. Yes, it was indeed Roderick Moore. I came across him stabling his weary mount in the Brackenthorpe stables and only my deep-felt guilt at my own mental callousness towards poor Edmund prevented me from falling upon his neck. I could not however suppress the surge of glad relief when I observed him to be whole and unchanged.

"Mr Moore," I said with unsteady primness, my hands clenched so hard behind my back that my nails pierced my palms. "I — I am pleased to see you, sir, and to note that you are — are well."

Roderick Moore shut the stable-door upon his night-black horse and gave me a level, somewhat quizzical look. He took a half-step towards me then halted with a frown.

"And how do you all fare at Brackenthorpe?" he asked harshly, only to soften his tone hastily and add pleadingly: "Beth — do not flinch from me in that fashion, child! I did not mean to alarm you — but I feel all is not well. What has taken place here since last I saw you?"

I held myself stiffly aloof for but an instant more then crumpled into tears of helplessness. He took me firmly into his arms and I made no attempt to resist — even when his rough, unshaven cheek pressed hard against my own tear-wet face.

"It was all so — so shocking," I told him at last. "Roderick — how can I tell you? You see, the Roundheads came — "

He held me from him with bruising abruptness and gazed urgently down into my eyes.

"Did they lay hands on you? Is that what is wrong, love?" he demanded. "Were you molested in any way?"

"No — not I," I assured him truthfully. "They came into the house demanding food and horses. In the — the confusion a fire started in the kitchen." I hid my face against his shoulder, murmuring indistinctly: "Mistress Haughton was struck down with shock and still lies helpless. Poor

Elizabeth d-died in the fire and so now *I* must be Elizabeth, or the house may be t-taken from us."

Gently Roderick Moore drew me down to sit with him upon the mounting-block. Slowly but inexorably he extracted from me all the necessary details of that terrible time. When it was over I was weak and wretched and made no demur when Roderick swung me up bodily into his arms and carried me into the house.

Cook was overjoyed to see our visitor and greeted him wholeheartedly as our saviour and the new leader of our small household. Her eagerness faded when Roderick told her regretfully that he would be unable to stay with us for very long.

"I am on my way north to Moorend," he explained with a troubled look. "It is possible that the Roundheads paid a visit there also. My mother may be in greater need of me." He paused, then added abruptly: "Beth — will you come with me to Moorend? I do not like to leave you here in this unprotected state. Come with me!"

Cook spoke no persuasive word to keep me with her but I saw her capable shoulders slump and knew I could not leave her to shoulder the burden of Brackenthorpe with only young William's aid. In any case — how *could* I leave? Sanctuary with Roderick's mother at Moorend would be a poor exchange for my lovely Brackenthorpe. It was not to be countenanced!

I merely shook my head at Roderick for my feelings ran too deep to allow themselves to be put into words. I saw his lips set mutinously against my decision. However, when he spoke to me again on the subject — this time in privacy — I kept firmly to my avowed intent.

"You are brave but wrong-headed, Beth Gaunt!" he accused me quietly. "The enemy will come again — make no mistake on that! Next time there may be no Captain Hardcastle to cushion you with protection. From all you've said, it was his presence that helped. But for him it's likely they would have put the whole of Brackenthorpe to the torch. You do not know that enemy as I do, Beth! Come to Moorend and make an end to argument. You will be safe there with my mother. Come — I can see you're wavering! Yes — come north with me now. We will be wed there Beth, and all will be well. When this war is over and normality returns I promise I'll treat you kindly."

He made no attempt to protest his undying love for me, to soften this cold-blooded invitation into wedlock. Giving an involuntary shiver, I fell back a step, shaking my head.

"Go home, Roderick," I ordered him in a tiny cold voice scarcely recognisable as my own. "My place is here at Brackenthorpe. I shall never leave here — *never*, do you hear me? My future lies here." When he merely looked at me, unmoved by my chilly tone, I added recklessly: "Go away and leave me, Roderick Moore! Edmund has asked me to marry him. When this war is over we will be wed and Brackenthorpe will be mine forever."

"Young Haughton has your promise on the matter?" asked Roderick coldly. "I see that I have made something of a fool of myself, Beth Gaunt. I had not thought to find you cruelly thoughtless of my feelings."

The expression in his eyes appalled and frightened me and I longed to unsay my hurtful words. Yet — how could I retract from all I had avowed? How could I smile and say I would marry *him* and leave my lovely Brackenthorpe, as if it were a mere *house* and not the focus of my existence? Something seemed to freeze and die within me as I watched Roderick Moore walk from the room and close the door behind him with commendable restraint. I could not find relief in tears for I discovered I could not weep.

He stayed with us for a further two days but did not attempt to seek me out for private talk. With a cold, lost feeling in my heart I saw him give aid and good advice to Cook, praise to the beaming William and a sympathetic ear to failing old Jacob. I sobbed inwardly for the loss of his friendship and many times during those two days considered reversing my answer to his unloving proposal of marriage. Only the thought that my doing so must lose me Brackenthorpe held still my tongue.

Roderick paid several unfruitful calls upon Mistress Haughton's sickroom in the company of either Cook or my silent self and I knew that he was at a loss how to help her — or us, with the problem. Both she and the maid, Kate, seemed to be wasting away from lack of proper nourishment but it had been all we could do to force soup or gruel past their lips. Kate was lying now upon a pallet bed beside her mistress and the twin burden they presented did nothing to help our unenviable situation.

On the morning of his intended departure, Roderick went in to see Mistress Haughton once more and I accompanied him. To my shock and alarm the lady was feverishly conscious and had found the strength to cast aside her bedcoverings. Her pale blue eyes were wide and staring and met mine without recognition. The bones of her face were sharply etched and she seemed almost fleshless. Roderick helped me to tuck the coverlet about her again and he propped her up with a pillow behind her shoulders. I drew in a deep breath, leaned forward and spoke to her softly, finding my dislike for her overcome by my desire for her recovery.

"Do you feel a little better today, mistress?" I asked her eagerly. "You must be hungry. It is so long since you have eaten! Could you have an egg, do you think?"

The feverish glare seemed to focus

itself properly upon me and I drew in a ragged breath. Death was in her eyes and I knew that my talk of food had been unnecessarily optimistic. Her thin, bloodless lips quivered and I bent nearer to catch her words, even now wondering if I might help her. When she spoke, I felt all my strength leave me.

"Bessie — *witch*!" she uttered on a harsh, rattling breath.

Her head fell to one side and she was ominously still, eyes and mouth slackly open. I could not believe that she was dead and that she had died hating me still. Weakly I resisted when Roderick forced me to my feet and propelled me from the room. We stood together outside the door of her chamber, his arm about my shoulders comforting, yet strangely impersonal.

"Do not feel guilty that you cannot mourn her passing, Beth," he said, holding me more firmly as I struggled to re-enter the room. "No — stay. There is nothing you can do for her."

I looked up at him, my lips quivering.

"She died with an accusation on her lips," I told him draggingly.

"I heard her, Beth," said Roderick quietly. "She is dead. She will taunt you no longer, child."

"You heard what she called me?" I whispered wretchedly.

Roderick nodded gravely and gave me a brief hug of reassurance.

"Cecilia Haughton was a bitter, hate-filled woman," he told me steadily. "Do not reproach yourself and never brood on what she said. Her spite has died with her."

I ceased my shivering, knowing he would never speak of what he had heard.

"Thank you," I said simply.

With the aid of young William and the indifferent, uncaring Jacob, Roderick Moore buried Mistress Haughton in the grounds beside her daughter. The maid, Kate seemed to have partial recovery of her senses once the news of her mistress' death was made clear to her. However she left the house one evening with not a word to any of us.

The unhappy circumstances had prolonged Roderick's stay at Brackenthorpe and he was naturally eager now to delay no longer before riding off to his home and his mother's side. He promised to give news of our undefended plight to the Haughton gentlemen, should his path cross theirs. He also promised to return to Brackenthorpe at the earliest possible date to check up on how we fared.

I bade him farewell from my usual place in the stableyard. I went with him quite openly, for the need to pretend my presence a coincidence was past. With a sob rising in my throat I realised that not only was there no Elizabeth to play the spy — there was now no Mistress Haughton to judge my conduct. I found I had to fight down an impulse to scramble up behind Roderick on Fury's broad back. Before he mounted he gave me a long and searching look, gathered me into a bruising embrace and kissed me fiercely.

"Remember this, love, and remember *me*," he said harshly, "when you make your vows at young Haughton's side. One day you will admit to the truth, Beth Gaunt. It is not Edmund who stands between us, is it?" He cast a disparaging glance towards the house behind us. "*That* is our stumbling-block," he told me with half-angry amusement, "that heap of bricks and mortar that you worship!"

He mounted and rode off without another word or a backward look. I was still, staring in the direction in which he had taken his departure. Then with a sigh that was half a sob I took my dragging feet and my heavy heart back into the house, to help to prepare a meal for the diminished number of inhabitants.

★ ★ ★

We were well into a damp and foggy November when Laurence and Edmund Haughton arrived home. Dully my eyes took in the fact that Edmund wore one arm in a sling. I had forgotten the Dream's telling me of his injury in the horror that had happened here at Brackenthorpe. I had no way of softening the blow which had fallen in their absence. They had not seen Roderick Moore and were totally ignorant of the terrible tidings. Somehow, I managed to stammer out as much as seemed necessary. It was not until they had digested the intelligence of their double bereavement and had visited the two sad graves that they ventured to view the damage the fire had caused to their home.

Mr Haughton took refuge in silence and shut himself away in his room above stairs, eating worryingly little from the trays I left at his door. Edmund, although he accepted the news less hardly, seemed to shy from silence, begging me for details, questioning me thoroughly about Captain Braddock, whose presence had caused the fire. I pleaded that he would not try to seek out this Roundhead officer with thoughts of vengeance in mind but he would make no promise to this effect. It seemed he found Captain Hardcastle also guilty and — unbelievably — ground out the ridiculous belief that Roderick Moore too could be held to blame. I would have been wise to have held my tongue instead of protesting Roderick's innocence.

"*Roderick* indeed," sneered Edmund. "You still have a fondness for Moore, do you not, Beth. I know his type. Doubtless he appeals to your sense of the romantic? I hope you did not allow yourself to be swayed by his — chivalry, in my absence?"

He was sneering openly at Roderick Moore and was showing less than his usual courtesy towards me. Although I disliked my cowardice in denying personal interest in Roderick, instinct told me that now was not the time to protest — not with Edmund in this grief-stricken state.

"These doubts and questions show a sad lack of trust, Edmund," I said, gently rebuking. "Can it be that you have forgotten you asked me to be your wife?"

"*I* have forgotten nothing," retorted Edmund scathingly. "I thought I had made that clear — yours is the memory which appears at fault, Beth!"

Angrily I wondered if he was already regretting his impulse to wed me. *Had* it been mere impulse, just to defy his mother? I had accepted earlier that his main reason for speaking of marriage had been a need to assert his independence.

We were upon uneasy terms of truce when he and his father again departed from Brackenthorpe. Yet I must have been wrong to assume his waning interest for his leave-taking was possessive. Kissing me half in anger, he warned that I should have a firm answer to his suit when next he saw me. I felt so out of charity with him that I made no move to help when his bandaged arm made mounting a difficulty.

Roderick Moore had also kissed me angrily. His anger had been in protest at my determination to stay at Brackenthorpe at all cost. Both Edmund and Roderick had spoken to me of marriage, I thought broodingly. Was I being unreasonable when I mourned the fact that neither of them had declared his undying love?

9

OLD Jacob died at the bitterly cold beginning of that new year of 1644. Snow lay deep upon the ground, there was very little food and we had felt obliged to bring Sorrel, our cow and the remaining hens into the comparative warmth of the hall. We were all suffering from lack of nourishment, from chilblains and from black despair. The old man gave up the fight for survival in spite of all our tender, if poor, care. We three remaining: Cook, William and I, dressed ourselves in several extra layers of clothing and plodded out through the snow, numb both in body and spirit. It would have been unwise to have kept Jacob's pathetic remains within doors for long, therefore a shallow grave had to be hacked out of the frozen earth. None of us showed much emotion for we were all past weeping.

That evening Cook asserted herself with an effort that amazed me, caught one of our family of hens and had it prepared for the pot even before it was properly cold. At any other time this would have revolted both my stomach and my mind. Tonight I spooned up my chicken broth as quickly as if I expected the bowl to be stolen from my hands.

Given these conditions for very much longer, my new inner warmth allowed me to reason, we three might soon be at the level of animals — struggling with each other for the last morsel of food. It was a dismaying thought. Made human at last by my first proper meal in days, I began to experience a fierce anger for what had become of us. It took but minutes for me to by-pass the war as reason and to place the blame squarely upon the shoulders of the absent Mr Haughton and Edmund. They had known that we were in dire straits when they had left

Brackenthorpe before Christmas, yet nothing had halted their departure. They had given more thought to the cause they supported than to us — the defenders of their home. The unfairness of it all threatened to swamp me in bitter self-pity. However, I refused to allow myself to wail at fate — and the Haughtons — and used all my energy to praise Cook for her good sense throughout this time of trouble. That good soul shook her head and gave me a worried look when I spoke. She sighed heavily and told me bodingly:

"I fear there must be worse to come, mistress."

I squared my shoulders and tried to smile.

"Worse — what could be worse?" I asked her, my tone bleaker than I had intended. "We have lost the mistress and her daughter. We have lost part of the house to fire — " I fell silent, knowing I had already broken my resolve not to grumble aloud. "We have suffered, Cook," I amended bracingly, "but we will survive!"

Survive, I thought hopelessly. How often had we used this optimistic word?

At last the snow began to thaw — bringing new problems. The roof at the end of the hall near the burnt-out kitchens must have been weakened by the fire. As the snow melted a monotonous dripping sounded and soon the floor was awash. We put the animals back into their outdoor quarters which were considerably drier than in here. Cook and I mopped up the water in cheerless silence and William did his best to patch up the crack. However, the ceiling was dangerously high and I soon begged the lad to come down.

"Better a leaking roof than another corpse upon our hands," I said quietly to Cook.

★ ★ ★

Into the chaos of our ill-fed, makeshift existence rode a small grim faced party of parliamentary soldiers. We were too numb with all that we had suffered, to think of speculating on what the Roundheads would do on this chill February day.

However their leader proved to be none other than Captain Jonas Hardcastle. I was relieved, if not overjoyed, when I forced myself to consider his presence at Brackenthorpe. His demeanour, though somewhat stiff, was undeniably friendly. When he exclaimed condemningly at our pitiable situation and ordered his reluctant men to give us salt-beef and other mouth-watering delicacies I found myself in danger of warming to him. After an excellent meal produced by the captain's scowling cook-orderly I was almost ready to fall upon his neck in gratitude. When he led me to sit with him beside the warm hearth and away from evesdroppers I began to wish I had remained a little more distant in manner with him.

"Mistress Elizabeth," he began, a softened look in the normal steeliness of his eyes, his stern features relaxing, "I have no words to express my true regret for all that has passed here since first I met you. Your lady mother is no more and your beautiful home," his eyes went thoughtfully around the hall, "has been unfairly humbled. Now I find you to be starved of food and comforts. It is sad indeed! I have a suggestion to make to you, my dear." He paused and gazed earnestly at me. "Under more usual circumstances I should have deemed it wise to wait until you were a little older before mentioning that of which I shall now speak."

I gave him a wary nod, still unsure where all his words were to take us. The meal I had just eaten and the welcome blaze from the lately meagre hearth had brought me out of my torpor and fully to my senses. Here, before me, with his gentle and placating words, sat the enemy — a would-be *friendly* enemy but nevertheless my foe. Fidgeting uncomfortably on my stool, I waited for him to outline what doubtless must be a well-deliberated plan. This man would do nothing in haste and without full consideration, I judged. When at last his proposition became clear to me I gazed witlessly in his direction. I could have anticipated anything but this.

"Ah, I see I have startled you, mistress," said Jonas Hardcastle, noting my obvious discomfiture. "Until you ponder on the good sense of it you must consider me somewhat old at over forty years against your youthful sixteen. I can understand that I have surprised you, my dear."

"But, sir I — " I began, then clamped my teeth into my betraying tongue. No — I was *not* only sixteen but I must not tell him that! He supposed me to be Elizabeth Haughton — not poor Beth Gaunt, the blacksmith's brat.

"Y-you do me much honour, sir," I amended carefully. "I-I hope you will wait awhile for my answer? You see, I am still in mourning for my — my mother and of course my father's permission would be necessary — when he comes home."

Jonas Hardcastle seemed satisfied with my halting words, brought me to my feet and pressed a fervent kiss upon the nerveless hand he held in his iron grip.

"I will wait in the knowledge that you do not hold me in disfavour, Mistress Elizabeth," he said. "As to your father's permission — circumstances may conspire to prevent his early return. It is this very unprotected state of you and of Brackenthorpe which has caused me to speak earlier than I had intended. You must not hope for the return of your father yet, my dear."

"Do you mean, sir," I asked him quickly, "that another great battle is imminent?"

I was told not to worry my pretty head on masculine affairs and sat down again obediently but my mind was reeling from this new and unexpected development. I had just received a proposal of marriage from this enemy captain. To all intents his motive was to aid my own protection yet, not for the first time, I felt that he was casting covetous eyes on Brackenthorpe. Did he think to own it through marriage with me — confident that the Haughton gentlemen would not live to return?

William had not had an opportunity to conceal Sorrel in a safe place and when the soldiers left us this time, they took my mare. I did not try to stop them, knowing that protest would be of no avail.

"Do not blame yourself, William," I urged with a consoling hand upon his arm. "Sorrel will fare better with the soldiers than with us. You know we cannot feed her properly. Come, smile at me, William! The soldiers did not take our cow, nor yet the hens and they have left enough salt-beef and other provisions to see us through until springtime."

William refused to be appeased.

"A soldier dressed in iron will be a

sore heavy load on t'poor mare," he protested.

As this unwelcome thought had already crossed my own mind I bit my lip and did not reply. Captain Hardcastle had left me a greater problem to resolve than the appropriation of my horse — loved though she had been. Another thought occurred to me then. I had not confessed my unwilling impersonation of the dead Elizabeth to either Edmund or his father. Suppose Hardcastle should return and ask them for my hand? My true identity would then be revealed. It was unworthy of me to have anxiety on this count when so much more was at stake, I rebuked myself quickly. Yet when the soldiers had gone and William was asleep I sobbed in Cook's enveloping arms and told her everything.

"Wed yon Roundhead captain?" she said doubtfully when I fell silent. "Eh — Mr Moore'd take ill to that notion!" Almost as an afterthought she added:

"I'd reckon as Mr Edmund wouldn't like it, either."

She could suggest nothing to help the situation. Bleakly I consoled myself with the thought that much could happen before I was obliged to face Jonas Hardcastle with an answer to his suit. The captain might be killed in battle. *I* might be carried off by a fever, for that matter! These morbid reassurances did nothing to cheer me.

It was warmer up in my slip of a bedchamber now that the thaw had taken away the snow. Cook had insisted that I kept up a pretence of being mistress of the house, ignoring my protests that I was near frozen alive up there and would prefer to share her pallet in the warmer hall. She had had her way and I had slept in solitary splendour with my pewter-ware as companion. The soldiers had either not found it or had not considered it would be worth stealing. Could pewter not be melted down to make bullets, I wondered confusedly.

I dreamed that night that I was in the centre of a triangle of ice. Three men were at its corners and each pulled at me in his own direction until I burst into three separate parts in the manner of a much-maltreated doll. In my dream the men were faceless. When I awoke shivering in the grey chill of dawn, I acknowledged them to have been Roderick, Edmund and Jonas Hardcastle. Could poor Beth Gaunt really possess the power to attract the interest of three such different men?

I shook my head impatiently to rid it of all fanciful thought. Dreams meant nothing in the light of day. I must believe in nothing of dreams — save in that revealing series of visions which I called "Dream". My mother had insisted that I name it so and I had had reason to be glad that she had so advised me. It still remained my secret.

Mistress Haughton had died with "witch" upon her tongue because she had hated me. Roderick Moore had heard her but had seemed to place no importance on the word. Earlier he had had reason to wonder at my knowledge when I had spoken of his wound before he had done so himself. I dwelled in detail on our conversation in the stableyard, so long ago, it seemed. No — I was sure that Roderick liked me too well to level any serious accusation at me. Witches were wicked beings! They caused cattle to sicken and die and children to ail from mysterious diseases —

I gave a gasp of alarm at my thoughts, climbed from my bed and began to dress hastily. It was time I went downstairs to help prepare our morning meal. Work would keep me too busy to dwell on horror. In any case, I told myself sturdily, I was *not* a witch and there was an end to it.

* * *

Reluctantly winter gave way to the warmer days of spring. William and I worked happily in the kitchen and new hope began to grow within us, even as our seeds grew into healthy plants. The despair of winter was behind us and it seemed that life would never again sink to such black depths.

The sunshine was warm upon us and our spirits gladdened. We scrubbed and cleaned and refurbished our clothing from garments in chests in the unused bedchambers. For the present I was indeed mistress of Brackenthorpe and paid no heed to a future when I must account for all my doings.

When a travelling pedlar-man came hopefully to the door I blithely exchanged a tapestried stool from above stairs for a box of cheeping chicks. William cleaned out the stall which had been my poor Sorrel's and we persuaded our remaining hens to mother the fluffy strangers. For the moment these new young fowls were profitless to us. Later, I exulted, there would be a plentiful supply of eggs. Our solitary cow had long been out of her winter quarters and was even now cropping grass as she stood tethered in the grounds. Looking past the beast, I felt a pang as my eyes lighted upon those three sad mounds beneath the trees. We had put old Jacob not far distant from his late mistress and poor Elizabeth. I did not brood upon them quite so frequently now that spring was here. I was alive again and felt as carefree as our newly-acquired chicks.

By July we had a fine store of butter, cheeses, and eggs pickled in Cook's special way. The apple-trees bore green hard fruit as yet but, together with the hoped-for berries from a bramble bush I had discovered, should provide me with jam and preserve ingredients by early autumn.

Into the midst of our optimism and new-found joy in life — a life quite isolated from our country's strife — came dire tidings one day. The news was delivered casually enough by a travelling-man offering leather goods for sale.

"Happen 'twas a desperate hard battle, mistress," said the pedlar. "Look at all t'leather pouches an' purses I've got here — will you not buy? Aye, t'Roundheads won, I reckon! Eh? Oh — on a moor somewhere's near York city, I heard tell. Aye — t'north's lost for t'King now. Malignant Charles Stuart, they do be calling him. As long as I've food in t'stomach and ale-money in t'pocket — makes no odds to me who's in power, King or Parliament, mistress! I ask you — what's it matter to t'likes of us?" He paused to draw breath, then rattled on: "I've a fair bonny lady's saddle in t'cart, mistress. Wait — t'will take nobbut a minute to get it."

I stared dully at him, my heart heavy at his callously told news.

"We've no horse for your fine saddle," I told him at last, "nor money to buy your goods. I'm sorry — there's no trade here for you."

The man began to bluster at me angrily for wasting his time and I was relieved when William strode into view. The lad was burly enough protection, even though he was not over-intelligent. Without a further word of protest the pedlar stalked off to his cart. I fled into the house, calling for William to follow me. We sat on our stools at the empty hearth and I looked from one to the other of my faithful companions, loving and respecting them both and delaying the moment when I must give them the bad news.

"A pedlar came," I said at last. "There has been another battle and this time the Roundheads were — were victorious. The man said it happened on a moor, not far from the city of York."

"So near — yet we knew nothing," murmured Cook, pursing her lips and frowning. She gave me a steady look. "Mistress, you're upset. Was there any ill news of anyone you know?"

I spread my hands helplessly and shook my head.

"The master and Mr Edmund were very likely to have been there," I pointed out, shivering although I was far from cold.

"There's yon Mr Moore an' all," put in William. "I hope as he's not been killed. I like him. He's a right good man."

Cook gave me a look, saw my pallor and put in quickly:

"Nay — don't go on that road, William-lad! Naught's happened to any of our gentlemen, depend on it! Happen we'd feel it *here*," striking her capacious breast with the back of a work-worn hand, "wouldn't we, mistress?"

I felt a heavy weight lift from my heart and gave a nod of agreement. Of course my loved ones could not have perished! Cook had referred to mere intuition but I had a power stronger by far than that. The Dream would have warned me if anything dire had occurred. Nevertheless it would not do for me to feel too optimistic. If the pedlar had had his facts in order and the North of England was truly lost to His Majesty — where did that leave Brackenthorpe, a declared royalist home?

10

ICE-COLD, I lay in my narrow
bed, willing my memory to recall
every last detail of the vision that
had just faded. My head was aching
in its usual throbbing rhythm but
still I persevered. The Dream had
painted a terrifyingly vivid picture of
a battlefield — dark with the blood
of those who had perished and rent
with the agonised groans of the dying.
I knew that someone close to me had
given his life upon that moorland field
of battle. Pressing a hand to my fevered
brow, I was miserably confident that
the scene I had just witnessed had had
connection with the battle spoken of by
the leather-goods pedlar.

I rolled over on to my face and
beat the pillow for a moment with
my fists hysterically clenched. Someone
had died! Who? *Who?* Was Edmund

now dead — Edmund who had left in anger and with no kindly last word for me? Burdened with guilt, I was still again and turned to lie upon my back. If not Edmund, then perhaps it was Mr Haughton who had ceased to breathe upon that battlefield? I sat up abruptly, my teeth hard in my lower lip. It could not be — it must not be — *Roderick.*

When it was time to rise and face the new day I struggled to appear normal — to act as if nothing new had occurred to shatter my calm. Cook had a sympathetic ear and was my friend but not even in her could I confide the fact that I had this magical — nay, *witchlike* — tendency to see visions.

With difficulty I put the experience behind me. Time alone would prove which man, if any, of my acquaintance had given his life for his king.

The summer morning was bright and warm when I went to the stableyard to feed the fowls. Halting in sudden puzzlement I stood and listened intently. Yes, there it was again — a soft metallic sound! It came not from the chickens' home but from the direction of the next, unused stall. Roderick had often put his black horse in there —

On tiptoe I approached the stall and looked curiously over the half-door. What I had expected I could not have said. Certainly I had not anticipated that I should find myself staring stupidly down the muzzle of a musket. I froze with horror, then fell back a step.

"Stay where you are or I'll blow a hole in you, girl," ordered a harsh but decidedly educated voice.

I did as the man bade me and stood rooted to the spot, gazing in frightened disbelief at this stranger who was half-kneeling, half-crouching in the empty stall. A ferocious scowl was on the unshaven face and the dreaded orange sash was about his stained buff-coat. Terror left me suddenly. An unhealed gash partly disguised the man's appearance but in spite of this I knew now that beneath the dirt, the blood and the ugly short-cropped hair lay someone I had once known and respected.

"*Master Anthony*!" I said eagerly. "Oh — it is good to see you, sir!" I held out my hand to him, ignoring the musket. "You must come quickly into the house. You will be hungry, sir, and that cut needs attention."

The erstwhile tutor, for it was indeed he, rose painfully and lowered his weapon. Under the beard and the grime his skin showed sallow and he seemed half dead upon his feet.

"Mistress Beth?" he said slowly. "Yes — I see it is you, Beth Gaunt. Who gives you leave to invite one wearing the parliamentary sash beneath the roof of a royalist home? Have you new authority?"

I spread my hands and gave a shrug.

"You will note unhappy changes at Brackenthorpe since you left us, sir," I said in as light a voice as I could muster. "Just now I am alone here except for Cook and William." I bit my lip and added wryly: "There, you see how unprotected we are here, sir! I trust there is no troop of enemy soldiers lying in wait for you to give them the signal to invade the house?"

Master Anthony opened his mouth to reply, then groaned and slumped down on to the stone floor of the stall, the musket falling from his nerveless hand.

It took the combined strength of William, Cook and I to heave the tutor's heavily inert form all the way from the stables to the hall of the house but at length we achieved our purpose.

William seemed as pleased as I to see an old acquaintance but Cook was greatly upset and nervous at his unexpected presence.

"Mistress, he's an enemy. Look at yon sash," she protested in a troubled voice. "Who's to say that more of 'em won't come knocking at t'door in search of him? I don't like it one bit, mistress — that I don't!"

Despite her grumbling Cook cleaned the angry cheek wound and fed her unwelcome guest with broth when he regained consciousness.

"I bring you sad news," said the tutor that evening. "I must tell you that Mr Haughton — Mr Laurence Haughton — is dead. There was a battle on Marston Moor not far from York. I met the Haughtons and was there with Master Edmund when his father died. I came to give the news to Mistress Haughton."

He fell silent, seemingly exhausted, and Cook and I stared, then exchanged puzzled looks.

"Did Edmund not tell you of his mother's death, sir?" I asked quietly. "Surely he told you that only the three of us are still here at Brackenthorpe?"

Master Anthony shook a weary head.

"I knew nothing of the mistress's death," he said heavily. "The Haughtons refused speech with me. Not for a moment would they forget I was their enemy. I fear that Master Edmund had to exercise great restraint not to attempt to knock me from my feet."

"You say that you *were* their enemy," I picked him up swiftly. Surely he did not intend to go on and say that Edmund too was dead?

"I am no one's enemy now, mistress," said the former tutor. "I will not fight again. I am heart-sick at all that I have seen and done."

"Where will you go, sir?" I broke in. "It would not be safe for you here, though I am sure we could hide you for a time."

"I have no need of Haughton charity," he retorted proudly. "You have a good heart, Mistress Beth, but do not think to gain aught for me from Edmund Haughton. In any case I will be long gone by the time he arrives home. Do not worry on my behalf, mistress. I am a tutor and, I think, a good one. Children must be educated even in times such as these.

I am sure I will find a position without too much difficulty."

"I do hope you may be right, sir," I said doubtfully. Who would take on a tutor with a battle-scarred visage? "Perhaps you will at least stay here at Brackenthorpe until you are a little better?"

"No, I thank you, mistress," said Master Anthony shortly.

I did not attempt to argue and change his mind, respecting his right to make his own decisions. Yet I was surprised and not a little hurt to find him gone next morning.

"'Tis for the best, mistress," said Cook stolidly. "'Twould have been dangerous for us to hide him here. Happen he's deserting from t'army, see? He'll not be safe or welcome wi'either side now, poor misguided soul."

She never spoke of him again after that, except to bewail his tidings of her master's death.

"Mr Haughton has always been both

fair and kind to me," I told her sadly. "I will miss him."

"Reckon Mr Edmund's master now," observed Cook with a marked lack of enthusiasm, then left me to attend to breakfast.

I wondered thoughtfully what difference, if any, there would be now that Edmund was master of Brackenthorpe. Would he still wish to marry me? A small voice at the back of my mind asked tauntingly if I still wished to be Edmund's wife. This was a question I was not yet ready to answer so I closed my ears to the inner voice and went to help Cook with the morning meal.

Some little time later, William raised his head from his food and said:

"I saw yon woman again — by t'graves she was this time."

Cook frowned at him fiercely and he began to eat, looking abashed.

"What is all this, Cook?" I asked in puzzlement. "Who is this woman that William has seen?"

"I don't rightly know, mistress,"

admitted Cook with a black look for William. "I think she's no more nor a beggar, or happen a thief. You've worries enough without adding to 'em — "

I was touched by her concern and not a little alarmed to realise that in her mind I was truly her mistress and not just a mere companion in distress.

"You should have told me about the woman," I chided her gently. "I wonder who she might be?"

"Chased her away from t'chickens last time I did," said William importantly. "Up to no good, I'd reckon!"

I was not unduly interested in the identity of this mysterious woman for it was likely that Cook was right and the stranger was just a beggar. It was odd though, I thought unwillingly, that she had never come to the door to beg for food. Who was she?

Two days later I was feeding the chickens, my mind busy with the problem of what I must say to both Edmund and Captain Hardcastle when

I had an opportunity.

"Ah — Bessie Gaunt!" said a cracked voice almost in my ear.

The speaker followed up her words with a cackle and I started violently, dropping my bowl with a clatter in the midst of the hens. My first feeling was a superstitious fear that Mistress Haughton had risen from her grave. Who but she had ever addressed me by this name? I turned and stared in bewilderment at an emaciated and completely unknown woman.

"Forgotten me, have you, *mistress*?" she said mockingly, then thrust her sharp-featured face close to mine. "Passing yourself off as one of your betters, are you? 'Tis Mistress Elizabeth they call you now." She sketched me a mocking curtsey. "Happen I know better, my fine lady! Bessie Gaunt's your true name an' *witchcraft's* your calling."

Suddenly I was coldly calm.

"You are Kate, her ladyship's maid," I said quite steadily. "I know you now.

How are you, Kate? You left us so suddenly without word. Why are you talking so wildly? Can it be that you are afraid to come openly to the house?" I drew myself up to my full height, which slightly exceeded hers. "Come — do not fear that the master will punish you for setting his home to the torch! You may depend upon me, Kate. I will swear it was a mere accident."

Ice-cold perspiration trickled down my spine as I waited tautly for her response. Her accusation of witchcraft had sharpened rather than dulled both my wits and my tongue. I rather thought that I had outmanoeuvred her.

"What are you talking about, witch?" she stammered. "I-I never burned t'house. *You* did it, witch! I'll swear 'twas you."

I regarded her steadily.

"But you *admitted* to firing the kitchen that day, Kate," I said firmly but gently. "Cook and William are here. They will back me up in all

211

I say. Come — what is your word against three of us?"

She stepped back further and curled her lips in an almost animal snarl. Relief flooded my whole being. I had beaten her at her own game!

"I've been watching you," said Kate next but her voice had lost its former assurance. "I've been living with my sister in a village not far away — "

"Then go home to your sister," I bade her firmly. "She will be worried by your absence, Kate. Go home and forget Brackenthorpe." I took a steadying breath and added: "Forget these wild accusations, for you cannot hurt me."

She cringed from me and I was aroused to pity in spite of myself. Bidding her wait here in the stableyard, I went indoors to pack her some food for her long walk home. However when I returned with the small parcel in my hand she had gone. Thoughtfully I went in search of Cook. Omitting that dread accusation of witchcraft, I told her about Kate. Deciding it was unlikely that the woman would ever return we said nothing to William and ceased to discuss her at all. The news of Mr Haughton's death still overshadowed all minor matters in our conversations.

★ ★ ★

Edmund came home to Brackenthorpe in early September. He brought only a groom with him from that small company of servants who had set out so bravely two long years ago, when war began. He did not explain where he had been since that fateful battle in July and I did not like to ask. His father had been buried in a village near the battlefield and a brief service had been read over the body by a clergyman with royalist sympathies. Other than this Edmund told me nothing of what had taken place. I felt that I scarcely knew him now. Gone was the friend and champion of my childhood. Gone, even, was that half-angry man who had asked to wed me. This Edmund was a cold and distant stranger. His first move was to allot rooms to Cook and William. I knew now that I had correctly judged his expression on arrival as disgust that servants should occupy the great hall. My own status as mistress of the house seemed acceptable to him but with a sinking of my heart I wondered if in fact I would ever become true mistress of Brackenthorpe. Since his return Edmund had made no reference to his offer of marriage — nor had he thanked the loyal trio who had worked so hard for his home. Cook and William had been my close and only friends during that difficult time. If I attempted to remain on these same terms with them it would appear that I must arouse Edmund's displeasure.

Cook was now merely the preparer of our meals. William's proud new authority was usurped completely by Bennett, the returned groom. When I made a stubborn attempt to carry out my kitchen duties and care for the chickens Edmund told me austerely that this was no work for a lady. The cold distaste in his tone almost caused me to berate him angrily but I held my tongue rather than endanger my position in his household. Regretfully I put my precious fowls into William's care. Outwardly I was meek and obedient to Edmund's wishes but resentment began to smoulder within me. His homecoming had spoiled our happy atmosphere — ridiculous though that might seem in his own house. We had managed matters so well in our own way before *he* arrived. I bit my lip to stop these angry thoughts from becoming speech. If I was to stay and be mistress of Brackenthorpe I must both please and obey Edmund Haughton. I must show in my every breath that I was a fit wife for him. It seemed I must go even against my own integrity and inclination. I did not love Edmund at all now and had to struggle inwardly to make myself *like* him but my determination did not flag. Only by marrying Edmund would I remain securely here at Brackenthorpe.

Roderick Moore had spoken the truth. I did love this house above all else. Yet, I must not think of Roderick. Such thoughts might sway me from my purpose.

Edmund and Bennett took daily rides about the estate, working to put it back into its former order — a task more suited to twenty than to two men. A mare had been established in the stables for my use but she was not my Sorrel and, childishly, I found excuses not to mount her. The war between King and Parliament might well have ceased for us at Brackenthorpe. It was evident that Edmund had not intention of riding into battle again. War was just one of the hundred topics on which we did not converse. Against all inclination I tried to force myself to adapt to the new regime and matters improved a little until Edmund arrived home one day with a maid for me. For weeks he had bemoaned the fact that I was unchaperoned and not attended in the proper manner of a lady.

I had to pretend pleasure at his choice of a maid for he seemed overjoyed to have found her again after all this time. I suspected that she had found him. Kate, for *she* was to be my attendant and close companion, was now dressed suitably if soberly and seemed quite unlike that haggard and demented crone of the stableyard. When Edmund left us alone in the large chamber where his mother had died — now mine by his own insistence and in spite of my reluctance — we looked warily at each other.

"Well, Kate?" I said coolly at last, "so you have returned once more. Was it your own wish that you should wait upon me?"

She gave me an unblinking stare.

"Why, yes, mistress," she said meekly.

It seemed we were each obliged to accept the presence of the other and an uneasy kind of truce existed between us. Yet I did not trust her and wondered how much time would elapse before that dread word "witch" was on her tongue. When I tried to discuss the newcomer with Cook our conversation was a one-sided affair. My erstwhile companion and comforter was now all too conscious of the gaping chasm of status between us — a chasm which owed nothing to me and one which she refused to bridge.

"Yon Kate was a good enough worker when she was here before, mistress," vouchsafed Cook. "Reckon a lady needs a maid."

Unhappily I left her. Nothing would ever be the same again, I thought soberly. Edmund's return had altered everything. I had not liked to speak to him even of Master Anthony's visit. It seemed, these days, that I was to spend a deal of my time in avoiding Edmund's displeasure and in speaking on innocuous subjects. However he mentioned the tutor one evening without any prompting from me and his tone was restrained rather than angry.

"Beth," he said. "I met Master Anthony some time ago. He was my tutor as a boy, you may remember?" I murmured something noncommittal and Edmund went on seriously: "The fellow left us to fight for Parliament but now he speaks of being sickened of strife and wishes to have done with war."

This gave an opening for a secretly debated question.

"Is this how *you* feel, Edmund?" I asked him timidly. "You have seemed different since you came home and never once have you mentioned the King's cause."

He eyed me musingly and I hoped I had not annoyed him.

"I am no longer a thoughtless lad, my dear," he said repressively. "Once it seemed the height of high adventure for me to charge into battle for the glory of Charles Stuart and now — "

"And now, Edmund?" I prompted, my heart sinking at this less than courteous name for our king.

He gave a weary smile, shaking his head at me.

"You always did try to probe into politics, even as a child, Beth," he said. "Do not be anxious, my dear! Matters between you and I stand unchanged. You are a lady and have no need to worry your head on unpleasantness. Let anxiety for the state of our country be *my* concern."

Unpleasantness? My mind picked out this one word from all he had said. Had Edmund no good opinion of my intelligence? Did he assume that I would not understand political matters — simply because I was not a man? He was speaking of a war which had cost him dearly and had not left me unscathed for I too had loved his father. Could he dismiss all that had happened as mere unpleasantness? Did I really know Edmund at all? Instead of obediently changing the subject, I tried another angle on it.

"Jonas Hardcastle has been to

Brackenthorpe again, Edmund," I reminded him. "He is a captain now in the Roundhead army. Have you met him at all in your travels?"

I wondered what Edmund would say if I told him of the captain's wish to marry me, then gaped in astonishment at Edmund's reply.

"Captain Hardcastle is a good soldier," he said shortly, "and please do not use that expression 'Roundhead', Beth! It is both childish and vulgar."

My first reaction to that was the regrettable one of wishing to poke out my tongue but I refrained from this equally childish and vulgar gesture. Edmund appeared to have lost both his sense of humour and his warmth of manner. If only he could be a little more like Roderick Moore, I thought yearningly.

It was some time since I had allowed myself the luxury of thinking at length about Roderick. I did not fear for his safety for I was sure the Dream would have warned me he had suffered hurt. I admitted that it would be very easy for me to love him and to say yes to his offer of marriage — even if he did not truly love me in return. But Roderick would carry me away from here. I had no alternative but to forget him! I had nursed and cared for Brackenthorpe through bad times and if good times were to come it was only just that I should be here to profit from them.

It was only when I awoke in the darkest hours of the night that I wavered at all from my decision and chose Roderick instead of Brackenthorpe. However waking to a new day always dismissed the night's weakness and my resolve was stiffened anew.

11

I HELPED Cook with the jam- and preserve-making that autumn but my heart was not in the work. Somehow Edmund's homecoming and his new disapproving manner spoiled my pleasure even in this task in which he permitted me to assist. Cecilia Haughton had always made her own jams and jellies, therefore it was deemed fit occupation for my hands.

Russet, the new mare, was a placid little beast and I decided at last that I must overcome my foolishness and ride her occasionally. Unless I did so, then Bennett must continue to exercise her. The groom was a sallow-faced fellow with close-set eyes and I disliked him on sight, not remembering him from the old days. He was not a Yorkshireman and his speech was harsh and foreign-seeming to my ears. Also he was overfond of inserting biblical quotations into even the most commonplace of exchanges. To me this emphasised his lack of sincerity rather than his godliness. In order to forestall his grumbling to his master of the extra stable-work I began reluctantly to take Russet out for a short excursion each morning. Despite the fact that she was not my late lamented Sorrel I found myself looking forward to this daily half-hour out of doors. She was a neat little chestnut mare and had probably cost Edmund a considerable sum. We never spoke of money but, as no further servants were added to the staff, I assumed that we were considerably less wealthy these days.

Since that damning name "Charles Stuart" had crossed his lips Edmund had said nothing to me about our country's state of strife. Secretly I wondered what would happen if Captain Hardcastle should call upon Bracken-thorpe with his Roundheads. Would he allow Edmund, who had fought against Parliament, to continue living peaceably henceforward? I suspected that the captain would be highly annoyed that the battle had not carried off *both* of the Haughton gentlemen! Would he still press me to marry him now, when Edmund stood between him and the possession of this house which he coveted?

Yet anxieties on this account paled into insignificance when I came across Bennett in close conversation with Kate, my unwelcome maid. I knew that the groom liked me as little as I liked him and gave an inward shiver. If Kate spoke in his ear of my practising witchcraft, what would happen then? Surely *Edmund* would never heed such foolish and unfounded tales, I consoled myself hardily. Truly, I had nothing to fear — had I? With a shudder I tried to concentrate upon anything rather than on the subject of Kate and Bennett's talk.

Towards the end of October I set

out one morning for my usual ride. The trees were gaily decked in hues of gold, red and brown and already were beginning to shed their leaves. Before long winter would be here again, I pondered as I reined in and leaned forwards to pat Russet's smooth neck. Last winter was now only a bad memory and I knew that Edmund would not allow us to fall into like state this year.

I was quite some distance from the house now and began to guide the mare slowly through the trees. When I turned to look back I could no longer see the chimneys of Brackenthorpe. A sigh escaped me. I was still convinced that I could never be truly happy away from this beloved spot. Yet — would my happiness remain unflawed if I were to marry Edmund Haughton in order to stay here forever? I halted Russet again and became very still. What was amiss with me today? Was I seriously considering that a happy future might not include Brackenthorpe after all?

Clenching my hands tautly on the reins of the placid mare, I muttered aloud in a fierce tone:

"I will *never* leave here willingly and no one will make me consider it!"

I had been totally engrossed in my own troubled thoughts and had not heard the approach of another horse. A sudden jingle of harness caused me to spin round in the saddle and stare wide-eyed in the direction in which Russet's head was already turned.

"Well met, Beth Gaunt!" said Roderick Moore gravely.

"*Roderick*!" I said in a tone of wonderment. "Oh — how glad I am to see you! Are you well and uninjured?"

My words tripped over each other in their haste and I felt a tide of hot colour rise in my cheeks.

"Well, Beth," said Roderick levelly. "Did you wed him? Are you now Edmund Haughton's wife?" When I was silent he went on: "I am surprised he allows you to wander from his sight in this careless fashion."

Part of my happiness began to evaporate and I looked down. Then, lifting my chin, I met his eyes.

"I am no man's wife, Roderick Moore," I said as I watched him dismount from his dusty black steed. In spite of myself I added in a softer tone: "Roderick — was it very bad, on Marston Moor? You look so weary and dispirited."

Mutely he held out his arms and it seemed natural for me to slip down into them and be drawn into their warm, safe circle. I felt him rest his cheek upon my hair and a new kind of happiness filled my heart — one I did not choose to question.

"Beth, love," said Roderick in a shaken voice, so unlike his normal tones, "it was like the depths of hell — the blood — the noise — the cries of the dying."

I tightened my arms about him, my only thought being a need to offer comfort.

"I — I *know*, Roderick," I said

softly. "I believe I saw a part of it."

He held me from him abruptly and grasped me by the shoulders.

"You saw it, love?" he said slowly. "You saw this in the way you once saw me injured?"

"Y-yes," I admitted in a shamed murmur. "Please never tell anyone of this! I beg you will keep my secret, Roderick!"

"So you *do* have the gift?" he said calmly. "I suspected that it might be so, Beth."

I stared up at him blankly.

"Roderick, it is not a gift," I protested. "It is my lifelong curse and leaves me open to accusations of witchcraft."

"Nonsense, girl!" retorted Roderick, drawing me back into his arms. "Others have had this gift. I once had a friend who possessed this amazing power. He was the son of my father's groom. He was my friend," he went on soberly, "and died at the hands of the Roundheads only last year. A vision had told him already how he was to meet his end."

With an effort I thrust myself from his hold and stared up at him. Absently I put out a hand to Russet's questing nose.

"You have met this — this power, before now?" I stammered. "Can it be that your friend made no secret of it? Was he not afraid? I live in constant fear that it will prove to be my downfall."

"As boys, Philip and I found it to be great fun," confessed Roderick. "On certain occasions we were armed with foreknowledge and amazed our adults. However I do remember that Philip was never fully happy with his gift. He complained of receiving severe headaches alongside each vision."

"Yes," I muttered shakenly, "it is so with me, too. Roderick — you do not think I am a witch, do you? You can accept this thing without accusing me of wickedness?"

He gave me a level look.

"If witchcraft exists, Beth," he said, "it has no part in you." With a change of tone he added: "Do you still insist you are to wed Edmund Haughton?" Bending his head to bestow a brief but bruising kiss upon my not unwilling lips, he went on: "Will you follow your heart, my Beth, or must it remain shackled to Brackenthorpe?"

I came rapidly to me senses, freed myself from his hold and turned to lead Russet back in the direction of the house.

"Come with me, Roderick," I said unsteadily. "You must come in and meet Edmund. Be prepared for his disapproval though, for he is a changed man these days."

In silence he followed me and we led our mounts to the stableyard. Bennett was nowhere to be seen and we entered the house, still not speaking to each other. Cook and William were working in the hall at the hearth where meals were, perforce, prepared. Even Edmund in his distaste could suggest no alternative cooking area.

"Eh, Cook, look here!" gasped William, who had seen us first. With a broad grin, he loped across the hall, grasped Roderick's hand in both of his and pumped it up and down. "I'm right glad to see you, sir!"

Roderick clapped the lad upon the shoulder and kissed the cheek of the laughingly protesting Cook.

"I am happy to see the two of you again," he said with obvious sincerity.

Suddenly I became aware that William had turned away and slowly I followed the direction of his gaze, to meet the cold eyes of Edmund, who had halted upon the stairway and was silently regarding us all.

"Roderick!" I hissed in warning.

He strode over to the foot of the stairs and began to give greeting to Edmund and my heart sank when I saw the expression on the face of the master of Brackenthorpe.

"Beth — did you give leave for this fellow to come beneath my roof?"

grated Edmund. "Did he come in at *your* invitation?"

"I — I," I protested helplessly, seeing Roderick stiffen, his hand moving automatically to his sword-hilt. "Edmund, are you not pleased to see that Mr Moore is well and has survived battle?"

"Mr Moore?" said Edmund, transferring his chilly gaze to me. "But a moment ago, you called him *Roderick*, Beth. Is the formality merely for *my* benefit?"

"He was your father's friend," I faltered, "and yours also, I thought."

"Thought? Then pray do cease to *think*, my poor dear Beth," returned Edmund with cutting sarcasm. He turned to reascend the stairs, then said across his shoulder: "I will give you ten minutes to make your last farewells, Moore — as a concession to my late father's well-known benign nature. If you are not gone by then Bennett will assist you from my property with the help of a musket!"

"*Edmund!*" I cried in shocked disbelief but he did not turn, merely went on back up the stairs and left us. "Roderick," I said in shaken tones, my hand upon his arm. "Please stay! Oh — this is so distressing! I will go after Edmund and bring him down to apologise. He must bid you welcome." I added stumblingly: "I did not expect he would behave so very badly."

"My dear Beth," said Roderick coolly, "we have now but eight minutes before friend Haughton implements his crazed threat. Come, love," he went on, confidently taking hold of my shoulders, "gather up such of your belongings as may be easily carried and we will be upon our way with all due speed. My sturdy mount will bear our double weight with ease. Never fear, love — a glad welcome will greet you at Moorend. This is no place for you!"

I fell back a step and clasped my hands behind my back tightly, the nails biting into the palms.

"Roderick — I cannot," I whispered

unhappily. "My place is here at Brackenthorpe."

He gave me an incredulous look and stiffened. I heard a murmur of distress from Cook and William. Drawing myself up tautly to my full height I waited for his condemnation of my stupidity.

"It seems I must apologise for wasting your time and my own, Mistress Gaunt," said Roderick with heavy, cutting formality. "I will now rid you of my unwanted presence, before your unstable — ah — husband-to-be spatters the floor with my blood."

He strode out, slamming the great door behind him. Without conscious thought I ran after him weeping, then struggled to reopen the door. He was already saddling his black horse when I reached him and the sly-faced Bennett was in the stableyard watching.

"Roderick — please," I said brokenly. "We cannot part forever in this shocking manner." I cast a look at the leering Bennett. "*Please*, Roderick, we must speak privately."

He led his great black mount out of the stall and for a desperate moment I thought he meant to ride off without even a word. I ran forward and put a restraining hand on the reins and looked up at him beseechingly.

"If I caused offence, then I beg pardon, mistress," he said harshly, then added softly so that Bennett could not hear: "Beth — if ever need arises, ride to Moorend. I can still be your refuge! Do not be too proud to change your mind, love!"

He shook off my hand (for Bennett's benefit, I hoped) walked his horse away from me then cantered off without even a farewell. I bit hard on my lip to stem a threatened flow of tears, walked unseeingly past Bennett and went straight up to my own room. The fact that Roderick had in the end reverted to his normal friendliness heartened me for minutes only. I stayed in my room in a state of cold shock until Cook brought me a hot drink in the evening. Her eyes were anxious and she was alarmed to have me weep anew when she spoke Roderick's name. Unhappily I turned from her and in the end she left me.

It was no use, I told my unresponsive pillow wretchedly. I just *had* to stay here and become Edmund's wife. Perhaps in time my need for Roderick Moore would lessen and die. He had told me I was shackled to Brackenthorpe and so I was — with bonds no one could sever. I no longer attempted to deny that I truly loved Roderick but the admittance brought me neither joy nor ease. Brackenthorpe was my *destiny*. Without love, I realised wearily, it could also become my prison.

12

I WAS not obliged to face Edmund again until we met at the breakfast table next morning and it was with some trepidation that I took my seat. He half rose from his own chair in mechanical rather than courteous acknowledgement of my presence but did not bid me good morning.

We ate together in silence. I found I could do little save crumble the bread upon my plate but Edmund seemed to suffer no loss of appetite though he made no attempt to meet my eyes. When he had eaten his fill he appeared about to leave me with but a nod.

"*Edmund!*" I breathed, rising hurriedly, so that my chair scraped noisily against the hall's stone floor. "Do not go yet, please! We must talk!"

He faced me across the table, pressing his hands upon its surface until the knuckles showed white.

"I knew you would not be content to let matters rest and leave well alone, Beth," he said with weary coldness. "Come then, *talk*! Shall we speak of your lack of loyalty, yesterday? Shall we speak, perhaps, of the way in which you favour Roderick Moore?" He drew in a deep breath and added chillingly: "I am bitterly disappointed in you, Beth." I sat down bonelessly on my chair and stared up at him. "Now, my dear Beth," he went on with a wintry smile, "be a good girl and do not upset me further. You and I have a bright future before us when this war is over and order comes to our country. Yes! Do not look so stricken, Beth — I do forgive you!"

I stayed upon the chair long after he had left me, long after Cook had removed the plates and knives from the table. A fierce anger against Edmund Haughton burned within me. He was so completely involved with his own affairs — such as they might be — that he had excluded me completely. How *dared* he forgive me? I was still his "dear Beth" who would one day be honoured by being made his wife. My hopes and fears, my very thoughts and being, meant nothing to him. I was of so little account that he did not even trouble to be angry with me for long.

Edmund Haughton did not know me at all, I mused fiercely. Perhaps I should have shocked him out of his self-sufficient complacency. Perhaps I should have told him of Captain Hardcastle's wish to marry me — of Roderick Moore's plea that I go to Moorend to his mother, eventually to wed *him*.

My anger faded as a new thought occurred to me. Suppose Captain Hardcastle should come again to Brackenthorpe while Edmund was still here? The matter of my supposed age and identity must then surely come to light. Should I tell Edmund now that Hardcastle thought me to be his sister? Oh — what a tangle it all was, to be sure.

While I was still seated at the table my thoughts left Edmund and the captain and flew to Roderick Moore. I realised that in confiding in him my well-kept secret of the Dream I had placed my future safety very much in his power. If ever he felt completely out of charity with me I had presented him with a formidable weapon against me.

Rising to me feet, I shook my head in self-condemnation at this unworthy thought. Roderick would never stoop to such depths as to use my confidence against me and denounce me as a witch. Even now, despite Edmund's unforgivable threat against him and my own determination to cling to Brackenthorpe, Roderick remained my friend. Why — beneath that unpleasant Bennett's very nose he had reiterated his plea that I go to his home, Moorend. I wondered about Roderick's mother. Had he spoken of me to her? Did she know that her son had offered to keep me safe by marrying me?

With an effort I put all such thoughts behind me and prepared for a brisk ride upon my mare, Russet. She at least demanded nothing from me.

★ ★ ★

Christmas was fast approaching but so far Edmund had not mentioned the fact. He spent much of his time with the sly, bible-quoting Bennett and spoke to me only on commonplaces — as suited to a mere female, I seethed.

Two weeks ago he had brought in some workmen and I had watched as they measured and muttered in the burnt-out kitchen area. However they had departed after boarding-up the gaping window-apertures and nothing further had been said. My hopes of a renovated Brackenthorpe had not risen very high for how could Edmund find a large sum of money for repair work in these times of war? I was pleased at least to note that he was taking a proper interest in his home.

The arrival of those workmen had upset my maid, Kate, although she took pains to disguise the fact. Knowing as I did that she had caused the conflagration, I did not wonder at her attitude. As Cook had pointed out, Kate was an able maid and did her work well. Even so, I could not be easy with her, remembering her demented cry of "witch" before she took up re-employment here.

When Christmas was but a week away and no preparation had been made I was certain that we were not to celebrate the festival at all. I was proved sadly wrong. This was to be a Christmas as no other of my experience. Cook and I had surreptitiously baked pies and cakes when Edmund was riding about his estate. We had also carefully checked and counted our matured autumn preserves. On the eve of Christmas day Cook muttered to me anxiously:

"Mistress, what's to do? T'master's not brought in pork nor beef nor suchlike for tomorrow's dinner. 'Tis Christmas eve!"

"I just do not know what to say, Cook," I confessed. "Perhaps the master is too full of estate business to remember that Christmas is nigh."

We were far from celebrating in the normal manner on the morrow. Edmund gave us no warning of his plans but we found ourselves ordered to rise early and, to our consternation, spent the entire day in prayer and fasting. I was in a far from prayerful frame of mind and was inwardly furious with both Edmund and that sly Bennett, who had doubtless instigated this whole sorry affair. Poor William was completely bewildered and was coldly rebuked almost hourly during that long miserable day.

"But I've just said my prayers, master," he protested uncomprehendingly. "When is it time for t'pies an' such? I'm right hungry!"

I voiced no outward grumble for I had the feeling that Edmund might take pleasure in reprimanding me in the heartless way in which he had addressed the lad. Setting my teeth into my lip, I said not a word.

Edmund gathered us together for the last time in the evening and I was less concerned with his words than with the conviction that my stomach was about to rumble in a disgraceful fashion.

"We have celebrated the birth of our Lord in a fitting manner today," said the master of Brackenthorpe heavily. "Henceforth we will join in prayer each morning and upon retiring. I fear we have become both lax and ungodly in this house!"

"Amen!" said Bennett devoutly.

When a troop of Roundhead soldiers arrived at the end of December I was not entirely surprised by the outcome of their visit. The soldiers took off their helmets, laid down their arms — with the exception of those on guard at the door — and proceeded to eat every remaining pie, cake and pastry we had innocently baked for Christmas. This was the first time that Edmund had been at home to experience a raid upon his resources. I hoped he would not lose his temper when his horses were led from the stable for the captain's scrutiny.

Little of this interested me deeply however. Every tiny vestige of my concern was concentrated upon one thing: would the leader of these marauders address me as Mistress Haughton? For this short-statured soldier with the weather-beaten face of a farmer was none other than Captain Braddock — he who had witnessed the burning of Brackenthorpe.

Ill at ease, I kept well to the background. Even so, I was close enough to Edmund to note the tightening of his jaw when the captain introduced himself. I remembered worriedly how Edmund had made me recount every last detail of that terrible day and how he had taken special note of Braddock's name. Was he now planning to avenge his mother, his sister and his burnt-out home?

My thoughts were proved to be extremely wide of the truth. To my relief Captain Braddock had only acknowledged my presence with a brief bow and did not deign to address me further. The soldiers were with us for a week. They made themselves very much at home and I was certain that this time they must have sought out every place where we had attempted to hide provisions. When I saw the last jar of blackberry preserve — which I thought safely concealed above stairs — upon the table I knew that I was unhappily correct.

Towards the end of this strange week Edmund called me to his side. We had exchanged scarcely a word for days and I was somewhat nervous. Wiping damp palms apprehensively upon my skirt, I wondered what he wished to say to me.

"Beth, my dear," he began stiffly.

"You must be aware of the changes within me." He went on before I could nod. "I have had much time for reflection during these past months and have been forced to admit the error of my thoughts and deeds. The death of my father has made me take a more responsible view of life. I am no longer a heedless boy. I am a man who has seen light in this darkness. Ah, Beth," he clutched my arms and brought me to my knees beside him, "pray with me, my dear, that you too may learn this great truth and repent of past wickedness." I could not pray for I understood little of what he had said. After a moment I was pulled to my feet. "I see you do not repent," accused Edmund sorrowfully. "You need time to reach this height I have attained." When I opened my bewildered mouth to speak, he stilled my tongue with a cold finger on my lips. "We will be married, Beth — *when* you are ready to acknowledge the truth. Perhaps when I return to Brackenthorpe I will find us in total accord."

I grasped at the one point I understood sufficiently to question.

"You are going away, Edmund?" I whispered, clasping my hands to still the trembling brought on by his strangeness of manner. "Where are you going?"

He dropped his eyes for an instant then lifted his chin and fixed his gaze on a point some six inches away from me.

"I leave in two days' time," he told me harshly. "I go with Captain Braddock's troop. I will ride with them to their command headquarters. I intend," his voice suddenly lost confidence before my horror, "I intend to offer my sword to Parliament."

For a long moment I looked at him, digesting his words in silence.

"You intend to ride with the Roundheads," I began carefully, "and return home to wed me when we are — we are in *total accord*?"

249

Edmund's brow cleared magically and there was relief in his smile.

"I was sure you would see the sense of it, Beth," he said eagerly. "For a woman, I find you quite intelligent!"

I could find no words to accept this gracious compliment but gazed as if I had never really seen him before. Indeed I found I was still bereft of words when he rode off in the company of the red-faced Captain Braddock. Edmund had pressed his lips to my brow in farewell and — ridiculously — given me his blessing. I stared unseeingly in the wake of the departing soldiers until nothing remained in my view but the frost-decked grounds of Brackenthorpe. It was William who brought me at last to my senses.

"T'master was a bit funny-like," he ventured, "but *see* what they've left us!"

A beaming Cook indicated the salt meat and other provisions left by the soldiery — bought by Edmund's change of loyalties.

"Yes," I nodded without much interest. "We will not go hungry this time."

"And, mistress," beamed William, "they've not taken your Russet, nor t'fowls, nor t'cow! Happen t'master wouldn't let 'em!"

I gave William the travesty of a smile then looked at Cook.

"He has turned his coat," I said with a shiver. "Cook — Edmund has joined the Roundheads. It — it seems so unreal," I protested as she led me to a seat.

"T'master's done what he thinks good for us all," said the woman, giving me an anxious look. "Now don't you go getting all upset, love."

I put my arms about her and wept upon her capacious bosom. When I was able I lifted my head, dried my tears and said shakily:

"Cook — how good it is to have you be my friend again!"

"Nothing's changed, mistress," she said reassuringly. "Till t'master comes home we'll go on as we did last year, just you an' me an' William — oh, an' that Kate," she added disparagingly.

"But *everything* has changed," I told her drearily. "Mr Edmund is to enlist with the enemy's army. Do you not *see*? Brackenthorpe can no longer be considered as a royalist home!"

Cook smiled bracingly.

"Ah, mistress-love," she sighed. "Does it matter at all — to us? It'll make things a mite more comfortable next time yon Roundheads call on us, think on!"

"Yet if ever a royalist troop should halt here," I began with a wavering smile, "think of our shame when they judge us their enemy!"

"Don't meet trouble afore it comes, love," advised Cook. "Come on, now, help me wi' t'cooking — a nice salt beef stew! I reckon that Kate'll be too high an' mighty to help us but she'll be keen enough to help us eat it!"

Cook's words reminded me that I had not seen "that Kate" at all today.

Suddenly convinced that she must have left with the Roundheads, I hastened upstairs in search of her.

"Are you looking for me, mistress?" came a subdued voice from the open door of Edmund's chamber. Quickly entering, I wondered what Kate was about. I was surprised when she bobbed me a curtsey. "I thought I'd best put clean sheets on t'master's bed," she said haltingly. "Should I wash these I've taken off, mistress?"

I eyed her thoughtfully.

"I suppose we could hang them up somehow in one of the unused rooms till they're dry," I said. "Kate, what is wrong?"

A flush came into her lined cheeks. "Naught's wrong, mistress," she muttered. "Happen I've just found out how well off I am here. I came back to do you harm," she went on, hanging her head. "Eh — I'm *that* sorry."

"Are we to be friends then, at last?" I asked quietly.

She nodded eagerly, more animated than I had ever seen her before.

"When I left here an' went to my sister's — well, reckon she didn't really want me there and reckon I blamed you and came back to do you an ill turn. But you've been kinder than I deserved, mistress, an' never said aught to t'master about that time when t'fire started — "

"You made a dreadful accusation, Kate," I reminded her. "I am not a witch, you know!"

"Yes, I know it, mistress," she said earnestly. "'Twas all nonsense. I did try to make amends, mistress, though. I've never told t'master how all t'soldiers think you're his sister. I've never told that," she finished with some satisfaction.

"That was just a misunderstanding," I said, wondering even now if she thought she had some kind of hold over me. "Matters were far from straightforward when the fire was under control and Mistress Haughton

254

was discovered to be in a state of shock. Captain Hardcastle and Captain Braddock too assumed that I was the daughter of the house. Somehow this mistake has never been explained. It is not really important," I said dismissingly. Then with a change of tone I went on: "Cook is at work with the meat left by the soldiers. Come down with me now. We will dine famously today!"

It took time for me to adjust to acknowledging my former adversary as a friend but Kate seemed sincere enough and I found it easier to believe her. Cook told me forthrightly that I was a fool if I trusted the maid but at least we were all more at ease with each other now. It seemed wise to accept Kate's explanation and apology and her new role as a member of our belowstairs community.

Morning and evening prayers had been promptly discontinued on Edmund's departure, to William's voluble relief. It seemed we had entered a happier phase of existence. Yet I knew I could never be truly happy with my poor Brackenthorpe forced into the role of a Roundhead home. If — nay *when* — the King and right prevailed we would be royalist again and so, I pondered sceptically, would Edmund. I was convinced he had joined the enemy simply because he knew the north was now lost to the King. How fervent would be Edmund Haughton's convictions when King Charles had been firmly reinstated on his throne?

13

OUR life reverted to the pattern it had taken before Edmund's homecoming — with the addition of Kate's presence. For Cook and William things were exactly as before, their life made simpler by the absence of their master. My own thoughts and feelings were decidedly more complex. My head ached with unanswered questions.

Had Edmund suffered a change of conviction? Had he, deep in his heart, turned his back on that royal cause which had meant so much to him? Could anyone change so completely and without regret? Yet, if affecting Roundhead sympathies was merely a move to preserve the home he loved, surely he would have confided in me?

One thing had become crystal-clear. I could not love this man Edmund

Haughton had become. He was a stranger to me now and I disliked that little that I knew of him. I shuddered when I recalled his words. Could I ever change my nature so that I became in "total accord" with Edmund?

The weeks went by without event and suddenly spring was with us once again. I looked at the leafing trees and bushes with vague surprise and my spirits began to lift. Smiles came more readily to my lips and to my amazement I was able to set aside the problem of Edmund's change of loyalties. Problems dwindled in this spring sunshine!

Looking at my companions with new eyes, I rebuked myself inwardly. My obsession with the dreadfulness of Edmund's action had been so all-consuming that I had not noticed how Cook had lost weight and was so much thinner that her gowns hung from her in folds instead of clinging to those former ample curves. William seemed much as always but Kate had a new anxiousness of manner which accentuated those lines in her face and aged her past her proper years. I judged her to be somewhere in the region of fifty — vastly elderly to me — but now she could have been taken for a woman of far greater age.

I was supposed to be in charge of our valiant quartet yet how badly I had neglected my duties of leadership. I came to my senses and made myself accept Cook's philosphy. As she insisted, it did not really matter to *us* whether Brackenthorpe was for King or Parliament — did it?

Russet's exercise had not been forgotten although this had fallen to William in recent weeks. It was very bad of me, I told myself critically. Russet was scarcely up to William's not inconsiderable weight. I spared a passing thought for poor Sorrel and gave a sigh. It was all too likely that my well-loved mare no longer lived. How could she have endured the rigours of warfare — she who had been so used to my tender care?

I took Cook to task for not eating sufficient food recently.

"I know our provisions have been meagre," I scolded, filled with guilt, "but I think you have been taking less than your share. We are all thinner these days but not as thin as you have become."

"I eat all I can, mistress," said Cook with a poor attempt at a smile. "I've had a touch o' colic here, see," she patted her stomach apologetically. "'Tis easier to drink than eat sometimes. Don't fret, mistress! Happen I'll be better soon. A bit o' sunshine'll do me good — 'twill do us all good!"

I stared at her for a long moment, trying to hide my anxiety. Then I went in search of a suitable remedy. To my alarm, the bottle I had labelled "for colicky disorders" last summer was completely empty. She must have used it all already. Cook could not, *must* not be ill! She had long been my friend. Oh — she must recover.

Eager to confide in Kate's ear and ask the maid's opinion, I began to look for her. When I had looked into each of the rooms now in use, without success, I was puzzled and began to frown to myself. Where could she be? I wandered out into the kitchen garden and gave an absent nod to William who was tidying the herb patch. No, he told me, he had not seen Kate at all this morning. My frown deepened and I went to the stableyard. Some of the fowls came clucking towards me, hoping I had brought food. They scattered, noisily disappointed, when I did not feed them.

Absently I stroked Russet's softly questing nose as she looked at me with gentle, liquid eyes over the half-door of her stall. I led her out into the yard and she danced good-naturedly in the spring sunshine.

"You'd welcome a nice gallop, would you not, love?" I said half-teasingly.

My gown was past repairing, an

ancient, ill-fitting one. With an exclamation, I kilted it up and climbed the mounting-block, drawing the eager mare beside me. Minutes later I walked her from the yard, then cantered out from Brackenthorpe's grounds and into the open countryside. Our usual morning rides had kept us within the immediate boundaries of the grounds but today I intended that we should go further.

A village lay in the direction in which I turned Russet's head. I had never left the Brackenthorpe grounds since the Haughton gentlemen had first ridden off to fight for the King. Today I felt confined and constricted and Cook's reluctantly admitted condition had left me sick and shaken. Perhaps I should have stayed at her side but I needed to be alone just now.

If the village I was making for possessed a name, then it was unknown to me. It was years since I had ridden this way. A wave of sentimentality threatened to overwhelm me and I slowed the obedient Russet to a walk. I could think quite collectedly of those long-ago rides with Elizabeth Haughton but not so steadily of her father. He had treated me as a daughter and I still felt his loss. If only he could have lived to restrain Edmund, I pondered next. Laurence Haughton would never have turned his coat.

The countryside was fresh and green. For a time we cantered along the bank of a stream and I saw the pollen-dusted catkins of the willow trees which bent their languid arms towards the water. In the distance I could see hills which would be clad in purple heather at a later season. Thinking I heard the song of a skylark, I reined in hastily and stared up hopefully at the pale blue of the sky. No tiny hovering bird met my eyes and the throbbing song had died and left me.

I rode on, foolishly disappointed. It occurred to me now that I knew so little of the wildlife of this Yorkshire countryside. Oh — I could identify a daisy and a robin and a bramble-bush but I knew little more. My skylark had probably been a blackbird!

Streamers of smoke, drifting upwards through the clear air ahead, warned me that I was close to the village. Once more I reined in and hesitated. Perhaps it had been foolish of me to venture so far from home. For all I knew, the village might be occupied by a troop of Roundheads.

Cautiously I pressed Russet onwards towards where the track widened into a trodden road. The mare was oddly reluctant and I knew that I shared her sentiments. We approached the blank wall of a cottage and stayed thus concealed until the sound of voices caught my ear. A vague, far-off memory reminded me that my last visit had been noisily greeted by a rush of dogs, pigs and children. Today it was strangely quiet.

In the act of dismounting I kept my seat on the mare's back. Yes, it would be easier to peep round the cottage if I were on foot but I would leave myself unprotected and unable to gallop to safety if those voices belonged to soldiers of Parliament.

Instead I nudged Russet nearer to the end of the cottage, took a deep breath and craned my neck to look.

From here I had an excellent view of the small houses. They had been built in a rough circle around the village green. The majority of doors were closed but I could see two that were open. In one doorway stood a woman with two young children clutching at her skirts. Her arms were protectively about their shoulders. In the open doorway closer to where Russet quietly fidgeted was a brawny, broad-shouldered man. Powerful arms were folded across his leathern apron and his face held an odd look of helplessness.

With an effort I dismissed these unimportant onlookers and gazed uncomprehendingly at the group upon the village green. I could see three men on horseback. They seemed in earnest conversation with the cloaked figure of a woman. Her identity was no secret from me. Indeed I knew her well. She was my maid, Kate.

These flamboyantly garbed gentlemen with their long locks, lace collars and fine hats were certainly not Roundheads. Yet, incongruously, each of them wore a steel breastplate. Yes, soldiers they were, but King's men! Excitedly, I clutched at Russet's rein, eager to join them and also eager to question Kate's odd behaviour.

Then I froze in the saddle as realisation flooded my being. Aye — these finely garbed soldiers were Royalists but Edmund's action had set Brackenthorpe against the King. Horror filled me. From where I was still concealed one of the gentlemen had a passing similarity to Roderick Moore. My heart leapt although I was certain he was not Roderick. I could not bear to think that these gentlemen were my enemies. However, if I stayed loyal to Edmund and Brackenthorpe, so must I consider them.

Impulsively I slapped my knees against Russet's sides. She anticipated my movement beautifully and we rode out bravely to join the group upon the village green. Belatedly I recalled that I was wearing my shabbiest gown and that it was hitched up to reveal my ankles but I lifted my chin.

The three royalists stiffened at my approach and became as statues but my first concern was for my maid.

"Well, Kate?" I greeted her quietly. "I had not thought to find you so far from home."

She cringed from me, her face drained of colour.

"Mistress, I do but visit my sister," she muttered breathlessly. "Indeed, I have spoken to you of her."

I gave her a nod and turned towards the silent gentlemen.

"Your mistress, woman?" asked one of them incredulously of Kate. When she nodded miserably he subjected the pair of us to a deliberate and thorough scrutiny and I had the oddest desire to laugh. Kate's cloak and such of her skirt that showed beneath it were far superior to my poor apology of a gown. "Your servant, ma'am," added the royalist stiffly.

The gentleman who had addressed me wore the red sash of his persuasion. Looking searchingly up at his dark, unshaven visage, I realised suddenly that he was deathly tired. A quick glance showed me that one of his companions had his arm in an improvised sling and that the other, a mere red-haired boy, had a grimy bandage beneath his draggle-plumed hat. The first gentleman was still waiting for me to speak and the other two seemed too weary to be interested.

"You are in sad case, gentlemen," I said at last, compassion getting the better of caution. "I hope you intend to rest awhile here and tend to your hurts."

Kate was watching me closely and I saw the mixed emotions which crossed her lined face.

"But t'village will have naught to do wi' them, mistress," she muttered. "See they've shuttered their doors. 'Tis not as if they're against you personally, gentlemen," she went on earnestly. "They've come to fear all t'soldiers. Last lot as came took all their pigs an' flour."

"War within a country is bad," said the royalist spokesman. Wearily he raised his hat to us. "Come, men, we must ride on."

I saw the youth with the bandaged head wince and was frightened by the pallor which accentuated his many freckles. Moved by pity, I said quickly:

"Sirs, come with me. My home lies not too far distant from here. We will make you welcome for this night at least and soothe your injuries."

"*She* said you have no love for our cause," said the red-haired boy in a harsh cracked voice, nodding to my maid, who refused to meet my eyes.

"For the moment," I told the men firmly, "*my* word is law in our home. Provided your stay with us is brief, we will make you most heartily welcome."

The gentleman with the injured arm spoke for the first time.

"May our Lord bless and protect your house, mistress," he said in a softly accented voice totally at variance with both the local speech and the tones of the other royalist. He gave Russet a considering look. "Your pretty mare is not built for two. Come," to Kate, "I'll suffer you to ride pillion with me."

Our ill-assorted party wended its way slowly towards Brackenthorpe and this time I had no eyes for willow trees and no ear for the skylark. My one anxiety was that we should reach the sanctuary of my beloved home before the red-haired boy slid senseless from his weary horse. I ignored Kate's frightened anticipation of Edmund's fury when this episode became known to him. I vow she never ceased her wailing all the way from the village to Brackenthorpe. How the gentleman whose horse she shared refrained from slapping her I shall never know. My chief annoyance stemmed from the fact that I too dreaded Edmund Haughton's anger, for this was his house.

William greeted our arrival with spontaneous, childlike pleasure and I went quickly to Cook to apologise for leaving her and to explain rapidly about our visitors. She seemed quite well in spite of her slenderness and went willingly for water to wash the wounds and for salve to soothe them. I busied myself at the cooking-pot, sparing a moment's irritation for Kate's idle hands. She was still keeping up her muttering, only in an undertone now. Our visitors must think they had come to a madhouse!

When the soldiers had been refreshed by food and care, Cook stooped to lift the empty cooking-pot, gasped and collapsed upon the stone floor, her hands clenched to her stomach.

The soft-voiced royalist with the injured arm was first to reach her. He shook his head, bade me keep my distance and called to Sir Harry Asquith — for so was named the uninjured gentleman I judged their leader.

They muttered together while I gazed in shock at my fallen friend. At length Sir Harry came over to me.

"How long has she been like this, mistress?" he asked me quietly. "I would say that she is seriously ill. Had none of you realised?"

I spread my hands hopelessly.

"She has lost weight recently, sir," I whispered, aghast that I should have allowed poor Cook to prepare and serve the meal to the visitors. "I have only just learned of her pain." I hung my head with shame, knowing that I had ridden off and left her today of all days. "Please say she will not die."

Sir Harry Asquith's expression was grave.

"We must make her comfortable, child," he said. "Are there pillows and coverlets above stairs? We should not move her now. Perhaps she will be more comfortable if she lies upon a bed of pillows before the fire."

Made angry by my feeling of guilt, I bade William bring down pillows from the bedchambers and shouted fiercely to Kate, bidding her help him. To my relief Cook seemed more herself when we settled her finally, according to Sir Harry's instructions.

The young soldier had not moved from his seat upon the settle and the new bandage was already becoming bloodstained. I went to sit with him, filled with pity. He was just my age, a farmer's boy from somewhere beyond Skipton and his name was Jem Field.

The gentleman with the injured arm and the dark looks slightly reminiscent of Roderick Moore was called Michael Flynn.

I never learned the respective ranks of these soldiers of the King but they stayed and kept us company for three days and three nights. When they left I knew that two of them, at least, were still unfit for travel. However Kate had rambled on at length of Edmund's embracing the cause of Parliament and foretold boundless fury on his return, so at last they took heed of her and prepared for departure, in spite of my urging them to stay till they were well.

I went to the stables to bid them farewell. As they mounted I pondered grimly on the many different horses, of both causes, that had taken shelter in these very stables. I could not even smile when I saw the indignant hens reclaiming the stall from which they had been ousted three days ago.

Mr Flynn took a small bottle from his cloak pocket and held it out with his good hand.

"Take this, sweet mistress," he said. "Give a spoonful to your Cook when her pain is at its worst."

"Oh — will it cure her, sir?" I exclaimed eagerly.

"Nay, m'dear," he said gently, "but 'twill take the edge off her agony."

When they were gone the house seemed strangely empty and I was completely forlorn. Cook was now fully dependent upon me although she was able to potter about her hearth and her utensils. To have forbidden this, however gently, would have made her miserable. William was his usual cheerful self and, as always, unafraid of work.

As for Kate — the woman set my teeth on edge. I did not understand either her motives or her loyalties and I was still not sure of her reason for being in that village, talking to the royalists. I found her presence completely distasteful. Had not my concern been all for poor Cook I would have turned on the maid, forbidden her the house and made her go back to her sister.

Before slumber claimed me on the night of the visitors' departure I pondered at length on all they had said during their short stay at Brackenthorpe.

Jem Field lived "somewhere beyond Skipton" and had he been in stouter health I would have asked him if he knew of Moorend, Roderick's home. I had been too much in awe of Sir Harry Asquith to question him but Michael Flynn had been both friendly and approachable. When I had known they were about to leave, I had gathered my courage in both hands and asked Mr Flynn if he knew Roderick.

"Moore?" the soft-voiced gentleman had said, giving me so quizzical a look that I felt my colour rise hotly. "Ah, so that's the way of it, m'dear? Now, Moore — let me see. Would he be something of my own style an'riding beneath Rupert's banner?"

I had clasped my hands eagerly.

"Yes — yes, that is Roderick! Is he well, oh, tell me that he is unhurt?"

Mr Flynn had shaken a regretful head for when we had worked out the dates we found that I had seen

Roderick more recently than he had.

I lay upon my bed, still thinking. I had dosed Cook earlier from Mr Flynn's bottle and left her sleeping. Wondering if perhaps she might have woken, I got up quickly, stifling all further thought and went belowstairs to see how she did.

I put a little more wood upon the low fire. My actions were quiet because I could see from the fire's glow that Cook still slept upon her improvised bed. On tiptoe I retraced my steps, doused my bedside candle and climbed, shivering, back between the now cold sheets.

Cook *must* recover, ah, but she must! How would we fare without her good sense and kindliness?

14

BY the middle of April of this year of 1645 the trees were unfurling their first leaves, our vegetable-patch was planted out and the call of the cuckoo was daily in the sun-warmed air. I hoped that summer was to come early this year.

To my heartfelt relief Cook's condition seemed to improve with the sunnier days. Mr Flynn's remedy still half-filled its bottle and was only used for the severest pain. At my insistence much of the cooking and cleaning work was now my concern. Cook protested at being left idle for a great part of the day but her protests lacked conviction and I knew she was glad to be relieved of almost all of her former duties.

Kate was still a puzzle to me and I lacked the patience to attempt to understand her. I could almost allow myself to believe her ashamed of her panic at the time of the royalists' visit and eager to make amends — if I gave her the opportunity. I caught many sidelong glances from her direction but whenever I looked her eyes were veiled from my view. She accomplished all the tasks I set her but was obviously not at ease. However she had none of my sympathy these days. That was totally reserved for brave Cook and cheerful William. The lad never had fits of the sullens or the miseries. He was always his own happy self, grateful for a word of praise, hard-working and enjoying his lot in life. He took no heed of Kate but spent his evening hours upon a stool at Cook's side. From his expression I knew he would willingly have taken her pain upon himself had that been possible. Although dull of intellect, William was a lesson to us all. I wished that I could lay claim to but a portion of his sweetness of nature.

We were just beginning to congratulate

ourselves on the length of time which had elapsed since our last sight of parliamentary soldiers when Captain Jonas Hardcastle paid us a visit. He was soberly dressed but not in armour, unlike the two helmeted troopers who accompanied him. He had come to see how we did at Brackenthorpe. I could see neither anger nor rebuke in his expression, so I was assured that he was still in ignorance of my true identity. He did not intend to batten on to our poor hospitality for he had brought provisions to feed us and his troopers.

"Mistress Elizabeth!" he greeted me, taking my hand and raising it to his lips.

"It is pleasant to see you, sir, and in such good health," I lied politely. "I observe that Edmund is not with you. I trust you bring me no bad news of him?"

"Ah, no, my dear young lady! To the best of my knowledge he is well. He has joined the horse-company of Captain Braddock. I believe you will remember him for you met beneath most horrifying circumstances. However he is a good soldier and Edmund will do well with him."

"I-I do remember Captain Braddock," I agreed in a whisper. "Indeed Edmund rode off with him — but I never expected that he would join the captain's own troop! I did not think *that* was in his mind, sir!"

"I must confess that I too was surprised," admitted Hardcastle gravely. "Edmund must have reconciled himself with the situation sufficiently to accept the leadership of Braddock. It shows a certain greatness in your brother's spirit, child!" He possessed himself once again of my unwilling hand. "Ah, I can see how this must affect your tender heart! I advise that you emulate the forgiving nature of your brother."

On inspecting Cook, Captain Hardcastle rubbed his chin with a horny thumb and told me that I must not hope to bear her company beyond this coming summer.

I gasped and clutched thoughtlessly at his arm, forgetting for the moment that he was my sworn enemy despite his present kindness.

"Oh, sir — you must not speak so," I murmured in distress. "She is my friend!"

He led me to sit beside him on an oaken settle, out of earshot of my companions. He took both of my hands in his and belatedly I realised that I should have avoided *this* at all costs. My fears were well-founded.

"My dear Elizabeth," he began, gravely earnest. "You are no longer a child. I feel the time is right when I must put the facts to you. You were born and bred a lady of quality yet you have shown your true worth in these hard times. You never scorn that which is menial and drudgery and you show friendship to all, regardless of their station. Now — there is little guarantee that your brother will ever return. He is young and headstrong. I fear I must tell you that men of his ilk are often the first to fall in battle. Nay, hear me out," he said sombrely when I opened my mouth to protest. "Elizabeth, my dear, Brackenthorpe is a lovely old house. It must not fall as a prize of battle, if Edmund is taken from you! I will not let that happen! Only tell me that we shall be wed, you and I, when all strife is over! I vow that together we will give back to Brackenthorpe its former glory."

A half-hysterical desire to laugh threatened to overwhelm me but I pulled myself together with an effort. Jonas Hardcastle was so deeply sincere in every word that I dared not cause affront. He would prove my formidable adversary should I choose to cross him.

"Sir," I whispered, "please do not press me now, I beg of you. I am very sensible of the honour you do me and I am sure I cannot merit your kind praise. You find me now," I spread my hands appealingly, "bereft of all my family and with poor Cook," my voice cracked, "at death's door. Do not, I pray you, feel that I have refused you, sir. Grant me time to consider — "

"Well spoken, my dear," he approved. "I like your modesty! There is no real need for haste. Indeed matters lie so uncertainly that there is as yet insufficient time to spare for the grandeur of a wedding that is your due."

I hoped he judged my down-dropped eyes as a further show of modesty for I dared not let him see the sick despair in them. If Edmund never returned, then Brackenthorpe must be supposed mine, for who could put my supposed identity to the lie? Yes, if Edmund did not come back and if Roderick Moore obeyed my foolish demand that he stayed away from here, then this insistent Roundhead captain might have his way. I tried not to shudder when Jonas Hardcastle's lips briefly touched my brow.

When the captain and his men had ridden off, I remembered Kate. Surely the maid must be my friend after all? She had held her tongue when our Roundhead guest had addressed me as Mistress Elizabeth. She knew that he supposed me to be Edmund's sister and yet she had said nothing. I decided I must make an effort to be more friendly and show her a little kindness.

★ ★ ★

The month of May was not far advanced when I noticed that the potion-bottle given by royalist, Michael Flynn, was completely empty. I held it tightly in my hand, biting my lip and thinking. A hand other then mine had dispensed the medicine. Gently I taxed the pale and wasted Cook with the matter.

"Aye, mistress," she admitted. "I've been taking more than you've given me. I've had to, see? Now, I'm prepared to meet my Maker, so don't you fret, lass." She drew in a painful breath, hands pressed fiercely to her stomach. "Happen I've no relatives left, mistress, so there'll be no one to tell when I'm gone." After an incredulous moment I burst into protesting tears. Cook tried to smile and raised one hand to touch my hair. "We've had much to bear, lass, you and I but I've reached t'end o' my road. Reckon you'll go on well enough, wi'out me."

She was lying quietly on her hearthside bed of cushions and I sat with her all that night and through the next day, letting William and Kate fend for themselves and refusing the food William brought to me. During the next evening my eyes closed from weariness and I slept for a time. When I jerked into wakefulness the figure upon the improvised bed was still and the hand clasped within mine was ice-cold. I could not believe that she was dead. Oh — I had relaxed my vigil for such a *little* time and she had left me while I slept.

For days on end I found no

consolation and read my bible listlessly. Nowhere in its pages could I find reference to a person unworthy as me, to someone who had slept and left a friend to greet death in loneliness. William told me later that he had dug a grave and laid poor Cook to rest single-handed.

"I said t'Lord's prayer through twice, mistress," he said worriedly. "There was naught but that I could think on, see?"

I put my arms about him and wept upon his brawny shoulder and he held me and comforted me as if I had been a baby.

"Oh, William," I said at last. "What would I do without you? You are a good, *good* boy!"

"Yon Kate's back," he said, relieved that I was no longer weeping. "Happen her sister didn't want her."

I had not missed Kate's presence and my heart hardened anew against her. How could she have deserted us in our time of need? Cook had been so good to all of us. I stiffened my shoulders, put grief behind me and once more took up the reins of our depleted household.

★ ★ ★

In June Kate brought news back from the village, which she still visited on occasion. There had been a new battle in what now seemed to us that distant conflict between King Charles and his Parliament. If Kate had remembered the facts correctly, and I had no dependence that this should be so, the battle had taken place south of Leicester — somewhere called Naseby. The enemy now had a trained fighting force called the New Model Army. In this greatest of all battles the royalists had been outnumbered and defeated, said Kate. Thousands of King's men had been killed and many royalists were now prisoners of this New Model Army.

It seemed sense to accept that this

detailed information could not all be set down to imagination on Kate's part. She had muttered something about an injured royalist gentleman seeking a night's lodging in the village and telling this tale of woe. I had to believe what she said whether I wished or not.

The truth of her story seemed emphasised in the worst possible way that night. After leaving me free for so long a time the Dream took upon itself to possess me once more. I saw this fierce "New Model Army". I saw blood and steel and utter chaos. I saw Roderick Moore and knew him to be dead for a sharp spiked weapon protruded from his chest. His eyes, wide and staring, showed no emotion for he lay beyond pain and anguish. Roderick was dead.

I staggered from my bed, sobbing and clutching at my throbbing head. Here then was the end of everything. I had loved Roderick — loved him more than I had ever loved anyone in my entire life. Why had I waited until now, until it was too late, to acknowledge this? He was gone — taken from me, before I had confessed my deep feeling for him. Fate's cruel blow had robbed me of a secret hope nurtured so deep within my heart that even *I* had scarcely owned its presence. It was too late. Roderick could never grow to love me — to make his matter-of-fact proposal of marriage acceptable. All joy was gone from my life. I would never see Roderick again.

If existence did indeed go on beyond the grave then one day we might meet again but that was chill comfort now. I had never pondered much on life after death. In those early, black days following the Dream I would gladly have made an end of myself — had I but been convinced that this could secure us a meeting.

Life was empty now and held little meaning. I did not stop to marvel that it should be so, nor did I question why this loss should be so passionately felt.

During the next days, following those

of complete shock, came the bitter, self-enquiry into how might be my present emotion had I accepted Roderick's proposal and learned of his death as his *wife* and not merely as his loving friend.

When at last I took heed of the anxious William and forced food past my uncaring lips, a further thought assailed me. What of Roderick's mother? In all my days of selfish grief I had not spared her one passing thought. I imagined this poor, bereaved lady to be small and indomitable, preserving Moorend from the Roundheads until her son returned and now —

Thinking of poor Mistress Moore, so totally bereft, drew me at length out of my morass of self-pity. Could I find it in myself to put Brackenthorpe behind me, saddle up Russet and ride to Moorend to declare myself the comforter of Roderick's stricken mother? The thought haunted me and kept me from my slumber.

Before I had properly made up

my mind Edmund Haughton came home to Brackenthorpe. Contrary to Captain Hardcastle's fear — or hope? — Edmund had come home unscathed. He was deep in plans for what he termed our impending marriage and seemed impatiently eager to stand at my side and take his vows. He appeared to see none of my distress, nor yet of my reluctance to discuss wedding plans. Had I not known him better I might have suspected him of feeling in some way guilty — yet of what? His manner towards me was many degrees warmer than it had been on his departure some months ago and his servant, Bennett, seemed now to be considerably less in favour than was I.

Edmund's calm reaction to the terrible news of Cook's death had put me instantly out of charity with him and I liked him less than I had ever done before. I pondered on the choice open to me. It would be all too easy to fall in with Edmund's plans, become his wife and have my position assured for ever more. This move would make me untrue to myself but did that matter now? Surely pleasing Edmund, whom I liked no longer, was more important than casting caution to the winds and journeying to Moorend? Was there any sense at all in riding north to meet a bereaved mother who might not even wish to know me?

15

"I BRING you ill-tidings of a one-time friend, Beth," said Edmund, some days after his homecoming. I knew that he was watching me closely and was thankful that his news was not to be the stunning shock he expected. I had at least been warned. The Dream had prepared me for what was now to be told. Edmund went on "Roderick Moore perished in the Naseby battle. I regret that I must be the bearer of this news, my dear, for I recall that you once had a fondness for the fellow."

I did not like to think how I might have greeted his words had I not been already in possession of the facts.

"He was a good friend," I said after a moment, with remarkable composure. "I am sure that he must have — have died bravely."

Edmund seemed taken aback by my

calm reception of his news. He looked at me unsmilingly for an instant, then went on:

"We met in battle, Beth, Moore and I." Hearing my involuntary catch of breath, he continued more assuredly. "We were enemies and I could have killed him, my dear, but I thought of you and I let him go. I did it for your sake. When later I learned of his death I was glad that it had not been at my hand. I could not have done that to you."

"You let him go because you judged him my friend?" I said quietly. "That was noble of you, Edmund. I-I do appreciate your gesture."

I was perilously close to tears and saw Edmund flush and look away.

"It was but an impulse," he said gruffly. "Never speak of this, Beth, lest I receive official censure. Captain Braddock would not like to learn that one of his men could be at the mercy of sentimentality."

I studied his down-dropped head and frowned.

"Edmund — how can you go beneath Braddock's command? He should be your sworn enemy. But for his presence Brackenthorpe might never have burned. The house might stand unharmed and your mother and sister still live — but for him! Oh — I do not know how you can march at this man's behest!"

"The bible adjures us to love our enemies," returned Edmund stiffly. "I must serve as my conscience directs. Do not begin to judge me, Beth. If you do not like my actions, then remember that I only do my best to serve you, my future wife, and my home."

Doubtfully I nodded. Nothing seemed to matter any longer and I supposed that marriage with Edmund was inevitable now. Roderick's death had left me uncaring of my own future. Why, in any case, should I protest at this chance of remaining forever beneath the beloved roof of Brackenthorpe? Had this not always been my aim? My hope of childhood years was made possible at last. How could I grumble against fate when everything I wished for was now properly within reach? Why must my foolish heart insist that I was being obliged to accept second-best?

Filled with guilt by the disloyalty of my thoughts, I forced myself to fall in with Edmund's wedding plans. If for nothing else I must love him for his gallant gesture in letting poor Roderick go free on the battlefield. I would have liked to have questioned further. Roderick's last moments on earth were precious to me. Yet what more was there to learn? I had seen his end all too clearly in my Dream. It would be foolish to plead for more detail and add to my heartache.

I schooled my emotions so well and so firmly that two days before the marriage ceremony was to take place I found I could face the future with equanimity, if not with eagerness. I congratulated myself on the fact that Edmund would never know how little I wished for our marriage.

Preparing myself for bed that evening, I pondered on the difference there would be in my status in two days time. Today, as on each day since Edmund's return, I had cooked our food and worked alongside a silent Kate and a cheerful William. Tomorrow new servants were to arrive and the day would be my own to make myself ready for the wedding.

It was late when I finally slept and it seemed I had had but an instant of slumber when I woke again. Slowly I sat up in bed and stared at the greyness of dawn through the uncurtained window of my room.

The pain took me completely by surprise and I clutched helplessly at my head, moaning at its ferocity. The Dream showed me little and was quickly past but it served to change my life. Its going left me limp and weeping. The tears rolled unchecked down my cheeks, hysteria took me in its grip and I laughed and shouted like a madwoman.

When at last I had myself under control I snatched up a wrap and donned it with shaking fingers. Barefooted I stumbled from my room and ran headlong towards that occupied by the master of the house.

"Edmund! Edmund!" I shouted, shaking him into wakefulness. "Oh — but you were wrong — so very *gloriously* wrong! He is alive! Ah — Roderick is *alive!*" When at last I fell silent I saw that Edmund's face was white and shocked in the chill dawn light. His eyes were wide and fearful and his lips sought for words they could not form. Realisation hit me like a physical blow. "Edmund — you knew!" I whispered hoarsely. "You have known all along that he was not dead. Oh, Edmund — how could you have done this to me?"

I shrank away as he tied a robe about his waist and threw back the bedcovers, coming towards me with outstretched arms, misery and suspicion writ large upon his face.

"Who told you?" he asked in a cracked whisper. "Who told you he was not killed? You know, don't you? But it was the only way, Beth! Moore is no good for you. You belong to me and to Brackenthorpe!"

I backed away a further step.

"No! No!" I gasped. "Don't touch me!"

"Beth, my dear," he said in an entirely different tone. "Go back to your room. What will the servants think? It is night still and you are not dressed!"

A sob broke in my throat as I fled from the room. My breath came in harsh, ragged gasps as I closed the door of my own bedchamber and pushed and heaved at the heavy clothes chest. I got it into place just as Edmund reached my door. I closed my ears to his plea for forgiveness and his entreaty that I open the door to him. Throwing myself down across the bed, I gave a shiver.

Edmund had lied to me. He had

said Roderick was dead so that I would turn to *him*. I had believed him for he had but emphasised what I thought I knew already. Yes, the Dream *had* shown me Roderick injured and with glazed eyes but now, tonight, I had had another vision. This time I had seen Roderick very much alive, though swathed in bandages. Edmund had said it was the "only way". He knew that Roderick had always come first in my affections and had tried to deceive me in that way.

"Oh, Roderick!" I whispered gladly. "Oh, my dear, *dear* love! You are alive!"

When I grew calmer I knew that I would have to face Edmund again. My chin jutted out at the thought. This time I would demand the whole of the truth.

We faced each other across the breakfast table and the sight of Edmund's guilty, shamed expression allowed a small measure of compassion to enter me. Neither of us made any pretence of eating the food upon our plates and Edmund gazed across at me in mute misery.

"What really happened at Naseby?" I demanded when it seemed he would not speak.

Edmund bit hard on his lip and seemed to be struggling for composure.

"Moore and I did fight together," he said at last in a tight voice totally at variance with his normal tone. "He would have killed me but I recognised him and cried out his name. He — he knew me and sheathed his sword. Later, he aided my escape. He did it because he believed you loved me, Beth. I told him you were to stay at Brackenthorpe forever and be my bride. He believed me and let me go — so that you were not caused distress." Edmund drew in a harsh breath. "What I do not understand is why, suddenly, you knew him to be alive, Beth. You appear confident that this is so — wildly and without reason. Naseby was Parliament's victory. It is all too likely that Moore perished shortly after he let me go. My dear — he just could not have survived! Do not stare at me like that — so accusingly!" He looked away and muttered: "I changed the tale a little so that you would not think me a coward." He gave a small, stiff smile. "Well, the truth is out! Now let us be more comfortable together, love, for tomorrow will be our wedding-day."

His eyes met mine. They were filled with pleading and I hated to see him so humbled. Yet, when I thought of how he had deceived me, I hardened my heart against him.

"Perhaps, in time, I may forgive you, Edmund," I said in a low voice, "but I know that I will never forget how you lied to me. There will be no wedding tomorrow!"

* * *

There was no way of informing Edmund's chosen clergyman of my decision and he duly arrived early

303

on the morrow. Hot on his heels came a detachment of soldiery. They were Roundheads and their leader was Captain Jonas Hardcastle.

"Well met, Mistress *Gaunt!*" I was greeted by the parliamentary officer.

My heart sank at his scathing, angry tone and momentarily I lost even that inner elation which had been mine since the Dream told me Roderick lived.

"Good day, sir," I said. "I-I see that you know my name?"

"Aye, mistress," came the retort. "I know much that you tried to hide from me." His voice was bitter as he went on. "How you must have laughed at me — you and young Haughton. I suppose you reckoned you'd keep your home safe — having a stupid old man like me on your string?"

I stared at him aghast.

"Sir — I never laughed at you," I protested helplessly. "Oh — I could never have made mock of your sincerity and — and Edmund knew nothing of this."

"Edmund. *Edmund*!" he mocked me harshly. "All the time you have been promised in marriage to young Haughton, when I supposed him your brother! And you say that did not amuse you?"

I drew myself up proudly to my full height.

"You are wrong, sir," I told him. "I am not to marry Edmund Haughton! Ask him for yourself!"

We had been standing a little away from Edmund and the soldiers and Hardcastle gave me a sudden, doubting look. I urged him towards Edmund. No truths lay hidden now, I thought with a shudder. What was to become of us all?

It did not take Jonas Hardcastle long to learn the reason for the presence of the clergyman and the reason too for his lack of occupation. As Roderick Moore was not mentioned, the parliamentary officer seemed to take new heart and sought for another quiet word with me.

"Mistress Gaunt," he began. "I do believe there is little fault to be found in your impersonation of Edmund Haughton's dead sister. I have given this matter my full consideration and allow that I have been a little unjust and hasty in my first judgment."

"Thank you, sir," I said quietly, my mind still busy with which course of action must now be mine.

He gave me a half-smile and nodded.

"I like your modesty, mistress," he said. "You sought nothing from your pretence, apart from an understandable desire to protect this house from occupation by soldiers of parliament. At that time you must have gone in great fear, for the Haughton family was deemed royalist."

"Much of what you say is true, sir," I whispered, liking his friendliness no more than I had liked his anger.

"I applaud your delicacy in refusing to wed young Haughton," he went on.

"I see that you must have realised you were unfair in marrying him merely for his home and not for his own sake. I like your integrity!"

I spread my hands deprecatingly.

"Sir — there is so little to applaud in me," I said.

"Now, say no more, young lady," interrupted the captain. "And look not so cast down! 'Tis not too late. You and I may deal happily together, after all. I vow I would make you more comfortable than would Edmund Haughton — even though I regret we'd never call Brackenthorpe our own."

Amazed by his eagerness, I fell back a step. The last thing I had anticipated was that he would still ask to wed me.

"You are very good, sir," I said quietly. "But I am no one and I have nothing. I am by far too unworthy of this honour you would bestow on me."

He smiled, his eyes so soft he seemed another man.

"No one? Nothing? he chided. "Come, Mistress Beth — I am offering you my name and my worldly goods! Now, I will say no more to tease you, child. It is growing late. We will talk of this tomorrow."

Escaping from him at last, I pondered unhappily on my position. Edmund was no longer my friend but at least I did not fear him. This parliamentary captain terrified me with his sincerity. I had expected his anger but not his friendliness and his renewed pleas that I be his wife.

I came quickly from my reverie when I looked across the hall. The clergyman who had come to marry me to Edmund had been baulked of his task and so had time for other matters. Just now he was deep in talk with Kate. The maid was an enigma to me and I was never sure where her loyalties lay. I was inclined to trust the judgment of my dead friend, Cook, and pronounce Kate my enemy.

In the act of making for the stairway

and retiring to my own room I found my path blocked by the clergyman. He was now alone. He was young and earnest and skeletally thin. I tried to pass him with a polite good-night but he stopped me.

"Mistress, we must speak," he said softly. "I have been told disquieting things of you."

I gulped.

"What has Kate been saying to you?" I whispered, turning to look at the maid who was watching from beside the hearth, a gloating expression upon her face. "I fear she is a trifle — well, *unhinged*, sir," I rushed on, knowing full well what Kate must have said to him. "She talks wildly. You see, there was a most horrific fire, sir, in which a young lady lost her life. Kate was here then. She has never properly recovered from the shock of it."

The young man nodded gravely.

"Yes, I have noticed the burnt-out part of the house, mistress," he said.

I drew in a deep breath.

"I see I must be direct with you, sir. Kate is my maid. She started the fire — oh, quite inadvertently — and her guilt has an outlet in an odd way. She tries to set the blame away from herself. She vanished from here after the fire and when she later returned, she accused me of — of," I bit my lip, hoping my rambling on did not make him judge me guilty.

"Yes, mistress," said the young clergyman. "She spoke of witchcraft. It is a terrible accusation for her to make, I am sure you must agree?"

"She cannot have quoted instances of this supposed witchcraft," I said, suddenly assured he attached no credence to Kate's spiteful words. "How could she — when I have done nothing of wickedness?"

He gave me a grave look.

"Mistress, I did not say that I believed her," he said quietly. "I merely try to warn you of the spite she has against you. She spoke wildly and, when she knew *I* did not heed her, she promised that tomorrow she would be more open. I thought that you should know of this, mistress."

Swiftly I turned to look at Kate but she was no longer by the hearth. In trembling tones I thanked the young man for his goodness in apprising me of her spiteful intentions. He said he had not believed her but he must wonder at what he had been told. No one could dismiss so shocking an accusation from his mind. I tried to smile at him.

"I am sorry that Kate has troubled you, sir," I said.

He bowed as I began to ascend the stairs.

"God go with you, mistress," he said quietly.

Once in my own room I sank down on to the bed and clasped my arms about myself to stay the shivering which threatened to overwhelm me. I had convinced Edmund, I hoped, that I would not marry him. I had coped to the best of my ability with Captain

Hardcastle's renewed suggestion that I became his wife. Today had taxed my strength and ingenuity to the utmost. Had I the courage to deal with this new danger? Witchcraft was a deadly, wicked business. If Kate did accuse me tomorrow before Hardcastle and his men, what would be the result? I had come to consider the maid of little account. Surely *she* would not prove to be the one to overset me?

I shed a few weak tears at my plight then firmly turned my thoughts to something happier. Roderick Moore was alive! Oh, Roderick, I thought wistfully, if only you knew of my trouble! Thinking him dead had made me acknowledge that I loved him and I was not going to retract that admission now. I loved him but that love could not help me tomorrow. Roderick would not come riding up to snatch me from danger and carry me to safety!

Thinking of Roderick renewed my failed courage. He had been right! Brackenthorpe was indeed only a *house* — a pile of bricks and mortar. Suddenly I was no longer held in its thrall. The time had come for me to leave! Unbelievably, I found I could countenance such a move without regret.

16

DURING the night hours I made a bundle of my clothing in the light of a single candle. My bible and pewterware must needs be left behind. A sense of urgency possessed me and I marvelled that I should be so eager to flee from Brackenthorpe. I had chosen a difficult time for my proposed flight and could see the sense of waiting until the soldiers left. But I dared wait no longer. Tomorrow, according to the clergyman, Kate intended to accuse me before Captain Hardcastle. Difficult though escape might be, I had to leave now. With the decision made I found I could marvel that I had stayed here so long. Could I really have countenanced marrying Edmund — just to possess this house? Brackenthorpe no longer held me in its power and the knowledge left me unsteady and uncertain.

I had only the vaguest idea of the way to Skipton but I knew that the journey would be too far for me to make on foot. There was never any question of my destination. Roderick had always told me I would be welcome at Moorend. Before now I had never seriously considered what it would mean for me to go to his home. I bit my lip. He did not love me, I was sure, even though he had suggested that I marry him. I must make it clear, on my arrival, that I was merely seeking sanctuary. He must not think that I had come confident that he wanted me still as his wife.

I could not walk so far so I would have to ride there. Removing Russet from the stable secretly threatened to be well-nigh impossible. Would the soldiers all be indoors for the night, I wondered. Would some of them be on guard in the stableyard? Well, I thought hardily, If Russet was not to be obtained, than I would have to walk — first to Skipton and then to Moorend.

Silently, cautiously, scarcely daring to breathe, I tiptoed down the stairway, the bundle of clothes bumping against my hip. I froze when a low rumbling snore reached my ears, expecting that any moment my presence would be detected. In the dim glow of the dying fire I could make out the still figures of soldiers sleeping on settles, on chairs and even on the stone floor. Firelight shone dully on their discarded helmets and breastplates.

Gathering up my last shreds of courage, I descended the final stairs. Before me lay an ill-lit stretch of hall, which had to be crossed before I could reach the door and effect my exit. I stood biting my lip and wondering. No — I dared not risk opening that great main door for it moved with creaks and groans and would serve to rouse the sleeping soldiers instantly.

To my left was an improvised door which had taken the place of nailed-in boards. Behind this door lay the blackened ruin of the burnt-out kitchens. Should I be so bold it might be possible to escape through one of the loosely boarded apertures that had once been windows.

Gritting my teeth and clutching my burden, I slipped through the shadows and slid back the new bolt that Edmund had fixed. It made no sound and within seconds I was standing in the dark shell of the old kitchens with the door shut behind me. Starlight showed through the unboarded upper windows of what had been the rooms above the kitchens. By their pale light I could see well enough not to stumble over any of the blackened objects that littered the floor.

Hugging the bundle to my chest, I lifted my eyes unwillingly. Over my head was but a part of what had been the ceiling. Up there, through the gaps in those charred beams, was the room in which ill-fated Elizabeth Haughton had taken refuge when the Roundheads first arrived. She had died there, suffocated by that choking smoke, and had been buried in an unmarked grave in unconsecrated ground — to be followed later by her mother and old Jacob and more recently Cook.

I began to shudder violently, almost forgetting the reason for my presence in this place. Yet somehow the time of the fire seemed so long ago. Much had happened since then and now I was being obliged to flee and abandon my dream of possessing Brackenthorpe. This hope had been mine for what seemed eternity and I was shocked to know how quickly and easily it had been extinguished.

I tiptoed across the ghostly room, imagining the scent of smoke still in my nostrils. My foot made a soft splash in a puddle of rain-water and I became still although I was sure that the sleeping men could not have caught so small a sound. Caution and care were necessary until I was miles away from Brackenthorpe. For all I knew, several armed soldiers might be abroad in the dark grounds.

Prying back a board nailed across one of the old windows proved to be unexpectedly difficult. I had no tool other than my bare hands. When a big enough gap had been made I had broken three fingernails and could feel a trickle of blood running across the back of one hand. My breath was audibly unsteady with the effort of working on those stubborn boards and trying to be noiseless.

I heard my gown tear as I scrambled gracelessly through the aperture and landed heavily on the bundle I had tossed before me. Yet nothing mattered but escape. Whatever came to pass, I must not be brought back ignominiously to face Jonas Hardcastle and Edmund.

The stables were very dark and I crept into Russet's stall with a madly beating heart. My hand flew out to muzzle her soft whicker of welcome and I rested my cheek against her velvet neck, limp with the effort of what had been achieved so far.

It was extremely dark in the stall and there was no moon to direct a beam of light upon my fumbling hands as I secured the saddle to Russet's back. Clumsily I tied on my bundle of clothing. I would have liked to have mounted there and then and to have trotted fast from the yard. However I was still not satisfied that all the soldiers were indoors and asleep. Surely a captain such as Jonas Hardcastle would appoint men to guard-duty?

Investigation revealed that Edmund's horse was there but that every other stall was unoccupied. For some reason or other the soldiers were not using the stables. No wonder there was no guard to be seen here. It was a warm evening. Perhaps the Roundheads' mounts were tethered in the grounds on the other side of the house? This was the only explanation that came to mind.

Softly I urged Russet out of her stall and, heart in mouth, led her away from the stableyard. I intended to leave by the entrance usually used by Roderick on past departures for the main gate was too dangerous.

On reaching my chosen exit in safety I came to an abrupt halt. Without a mounting-block how was I to get into the saddle? After many unsuccessful attempts to haul myself up I achieved my aim at last. For the first time, I was glad she was not the high-spirited Sorrel, who would have pranced unmanageably.

At first I walked Russet outside the walls of Brackenthorpe for I knew I had to ride towards the village. Skipton lay somewhere beyond there — how many miles beyond, I did not care to wonder.

Although there had been no dogs on my last visit, I skirted the village in case one had been since acquired and gave voice to my presence. Tomorrow I would be missed and, if at all possible, I must try to travel unobserved. The night was dark except for the twinkling stars in the blackness of the sky. Our progress was necessarily slow for I had no wish to have Russet set her foot in a rabbit-hole.

At one point I drew her to a halt, frowning to myself and listening intently. Was I being followed? Had I been missed already, I thought in quick despair. Those distant sounds in the night air were remarkably like the hoofbeats of a horse coming up fast in my wake.

Speedily I turned Russet behind a clump of half-grown hawthorn bushes. Thus concealed, I waited as the hoofbeats drew nearer. The horse came past my hiding-place and to my horror slowed and then halted. I was lying along Russet's neck, trying to muzzle her from making a sound but she tossed her head and gave a soft whinney of welcome.

Ice-cold, I sat up straight in the saddle. I had been discovered. I would be taken back to Brackenthorpe and would never now reach Roderick Moore's Moorend. The horseman rounded the bushes and I lifted my chin to face him.

"Eh, mistress, I reckoned as I'd never catch up wi' you!" protested a well-known voice.

"William!" I breathed. "Oh, *William*! Oh, how glad I am to see you!"

Had we not been on horseback I would have thrown my arms about him and kissed him soundly.

"Why didn't you tell me you were leaving tonight, mistress?" asked William indignantly as he dismounted and came up close to Russet's side. "I reckoned you'd be going soon. We should have planned it together, see? As it is I've nobbut brought a bit o' food an' a couple o' blankets. I'd have been better prepared if you'd warned me, like! Eh, I was that put out when I saw you'd gone wi'out me!"

Never before had I heard William speak at such great and lucid length. When he fell silent my mouth was wide open with shock. Then in a stunned voice I observed:

"William, you've stolen Edmund's horse!"

"Nay," he retorted. "Happen I've just borrowed it. An' think on, mistress, Mr Haughton's paid me no wages for months."

I gaped at this new forthright William, then slid down from the saddle, flung out my arms and hugged him.

"William," I said with a catch in my voice, "you have stolen — borrowed Edmund Haughton's horse and brought food and blankets, just to help me?"

He looked puzzled.

"Well — didn't I do right?" he asked. "Brackenthorpe's changed. 'Tis a bad place for us now, mistress. Happen you'll need my help. 'Tis a long, hard ride to Mr Moore's house."

I was astonished.

"Do you know the way?" I asked him respectfully.

"No more than you do, mistress," he grinned. "I'm right, then? I knew we'd be going to Moorend. Mr Moore said as how I must go wi' you when t'time came. He said go to t'Brown Bull inn t'other side o'Skipton and then ask for Moorend. Never fear — we'll get there safe an' sound!"

I did not know whether to be glad or annoyed that Roderick had been so sure I would go to his home eventually. William had been given his orders for the time when I decided to leave Brackenthorpe. How could Roderick have been so certain that I would accept his offer of sanctuary?

Stifling a sigh, I smiled at William.

"Come then," I said. "Help me up into the saddle and then we'll ride for Skipton. Some day I will reward you, William — depend on it!"

"Happen I'm nobbut doing my duty," grinned William. "Anyhow, Mr Moore said as how there'd be a job waiting for me at Moorend!"

In silence we jogged on through the night. At William's suggestion we tethered the horses, wrapped ourselves in blankets and snatched a few hours sleep in a concealing wood during the next day. If we were being followed, then we would make our track a difficult one to detect. It was new and surprising for me to rely so trustfully on William's judgment but I depended on him entirely during that long ride to Skipton town.

I hid with the horses and let William go on foot to seek out the Brown Bull inn. He was gone longer than I had anticipated and I had become quite sick with fear by the time he returned. I could tell from his expression that all was not well.

"Couldn't you find out the way to Moorend?" I asked, hoping that this proved to be the full extent of the problem.

William gave me a worried look.

"They said at t'inn that Roundheads have been to Moorend an' that some o' t'servants were shot an' that Mr Moore's lady mother has vanished."

A chill descended on my heart.

"Is Mr Moore at home, William?" I

asked at length. "Did they tell you that at the inn?"

He shook his head and lost all of his new-found assurance.

"What are we going to do, mistress?" he moaned.

I squared my shoulders and patted him on the arm.

"We will ride straight to Moorend," I told him firmly. "Even if the soldiers are still there we will come to no harm. Come, smile at me, William! You have brought me so far in safety. Now we must go on to Mr Moore's home, exactly as we planned. If no one is there, then we must wait. He visits his home whenever it is possible." William continued to look at me doubtfully, so I added bracingly: "If some of the servants are hurt, they may need our help."

I did not like to speculate on the fate of the missing Mistress Moore but possibly we might find her safe and well.

Moorend to my untutored eyes appeared a small castle. It perched upon a steep outcrop of rock and below was a still, silent lake — or tarn, as I knew I should call it. William and I reined in our horses on the track beside the tarn and shaded our eyes against the sun to gaze upwards at the home of Roderick Moore. It was obviously of far greater antiquity than Brackenthorpe and I felt my interest quicken, even though I had already been determined to like anything that was Roderick's.

The track wound steeply upwards, scarcely more than a carriage-width in places. Once the tarn was behind us purple-heathered moorland and tufted bracken were to left and right of our horses. The air was cool and invigorating even on this summer's day and Moorend grew steadily nearer, etched against the blue brilliance of the sky.

At last we reached the gates, to find

them wide open. Slowly we urged our mounts to pick their way into a central courtyard round which was built the house. The sound of our hoofbeats were followed by an eerie succession of echoes in the enclosed yard.

"Nobody's here, mistress," said William, looking round in disappointment. "Happen t'Roundheads have killed everybody."

"Oh, hush, William!" I snapped, made angry by my own alarm. "Come, let us stable our horses. Of course there must be someone here!"

The stables were empty of horses but it was evident that they had been occupied quite recently. It seemed ominous that the stalls had not been cleaned out. Who had used them last? Roundheads? Surely William was not correct. Could it really be that no one was left alive at Moorend? Slowly we came back out into the sunlight and I shivered though it was warm in the enclosed courtyard.

"Mistress," said William suddenly,

making me start in alarm, "will Mr Edmund have me hanged as a horse-thief?"

I gave a shaky laugh.

"William — what a time to think of that!" I said. "No, of course Edmund would not think of such a thing. He will know that you are with me," I said with no real assurance. "William — we must go into the house. It is possible that our arrival has been noted and that people are hiding within doors."

I took his unwilling arm and made him accompany me up to the big main door. I rapped loudly and then waited. At length I took the handle tentatively and felt it move beneath my fingers.

"Is — is any one there?" I called through the now open door.

Silence greeted my words and I turned to grab William's arm for he was beginning to retreat. Unwillingly he followed me over the threshold. We found ourselves in a high-roofed hall with a large, empty hearth in the wall opposite. Closed doors lay to left and right. Sunlight slanted in through small-paned windows and shone dismally on the dead ashes in the hearth.

"They're all dead!" gabbled William in superstitious fear. "Mistress — let's get away while we can!"

"Don't be foolish!" I said crossly, ignoring the rapid hammering of my heart. Drawing in a quick breath and bracing myself, I shouted at the full pitch of my lungs:

"Mistress Moore! Where are you? I am a friend of your son!"

William was almost back in the courtyard, when a door opened suddenly and an elderly man in servant's garb came into the hall. He stared across, seeming as much afraid as my cowardly companion.

"Good-day to you, ma'am," he said with a nervous little bow. "What is your business here, please?"

"Is Mistress Moore at home?" I asked eagerly. "I am Beth Gaunt. I am a friend of your master. That great fellow, shivering in his shoes, is

331

William, my companion. We are from Brackenthorpe."

A slow smile began upon that elderly face and the man took a step forward.

"Mistress Gaunt! We have heard of you. Please, I will see if my mistress is — is here."

He left the room and gladness filled me. Roderick's mother was alive at least! I lifted my chin and clenched my hands in half-anxious anticipation of meeting her. Suppose she did not like me? Suppose she wished I had not come? Suppose — ?

"Beth! Oh, my dear — at *last*!"

I was enfolded in warm arms and a kiss was planted soundly upon my cheek. Mistress Moore had not waited for the servant to announce her presence. She had entered the hall almost at a run and all my doubts had fled.

"I am happy to meet you," I said shyly.

She held me at arm's length and studied me intently from my dusty shoes to my dishevelled hair, then wiped a tear from her eye. In turn I studied her. Those eyes were of the same deep blue as were her son's. Indeed she was very like him, except for her snow-white hair. In spite of that hair I saw that she was younger than I had anticipated.

She drew me with her into the next room and we left William with the elderly retainer. They would hide our horses, she told me. The stables were not safe. It was all too likely that the Roundheads would return.

"Have you news of Roderick, ma'am?" I asked. "I thought he was dead but then learned that he was still alive and injured."

"He told me of your Gift," said Mistress Moore. "Come, do not flinch from me, child! He warned me you had the idea everyone would think you a witch! I hope you do not mind that he told me? You see, he has told me so much about you. He loves you dearly, Beth, but should have told you so himself. Yes, he confided that in me also. He bade you choose between himself and your home and adoptive family and could not understand your indecision. How like a man!"

"But he said he would marry me to keep me safe," I whispered. "He never spoke of love, ma'am! He met Edmund Haughton in battle and let Edmund go free to — to marry me. Edmund has admitted it. If I had thought that Roderick loved me I might have come here sooner."

She shook her head at the tears trickling helplessly down my cheeks and took my cold hands in her warm ones.

"Ah, do not weep, child! All is not lost! You must go to Roderick and tell him you do not love this Edmund Haughton. It is all a foolish misunderstanding! Roderick is here at Moorend. How he managed to ride home so badly injured was little short of a miracle. His condition is a little better now and I am sure his recovery

will be complete when he sees you!"
She smiled at my stupefied expression.
"If you love my son," she said gently,
"then come with me and tell him so!"

I dashed the tears from my eyes
and followed her across the room to
a wall which was completely covered
by a tapestry hanging. It depicted
the prophet Elijah being fed by the
ravens. My heart was beating rapidly in
anticipation of meeting Roderick in the
knowledge that he loved me. I had let
him think I preferred Brackenthorpe's
bricks and mortar to him. Would he
ever forgive me?

There was no door behind the
tapestry and, fascinated, I watched
Mistress Moore as she pushed and
heaved against the large blocks of stone
from which the wall was constructed.
Before my wide-eyed gaze an aperture
appeared. It was something the size of
a low door. The lady beckoned and
obediently I ducked my head and
followed her into the void. It was very
dark and she made me squeeze myself

past her while she closed up the entry. I was glad of the hand she offered and stumbled in her wake down a flight of rough-hewn, unseen stairs.

At the foot of these steep and narrow stairs was a door leading into a small hidden chamber. It was well illuminated by a branch of candles. A young servant-boy rose from his chair to greet us, his eyes curiously turned to me.

Roderick lay upon a low pallet bed, his eyes closed and a ragged growth of beard disguising his usual appearance. A bulky bandage swathed his chest. Wordlessly I fell on my knees beside the bed and possessed myself of one of his limp hands. Mistress Moore and the boy left the small room quietly.

"Oh, Roderick, Roderick!" I whispered. "I have left Brackenthorpe, as you said I would. Please do not send me away! I love you and your mother says you love me too. I thought you were only sorry for me. Oh, sleep well and recover your strength."

I must have slept for when I next opened my eyes the candles were guttering in their sockets and my knees were so cramped I could scarcely move. Roderick's hand was still in mine and he was awake.

"I thought you would sleep for ever, Beth!" he told me. "So you came at last. Did William bring you, as I ordered?"

Quickly I freed my hand and rose to my feet.

"You were very sure that I would come to you in the end, weren't you?" I said quietly.

"The only thing I have ever been sure of," he began, trying to lift his head, than falling back with a gasp of pain, "is my own feeling for *you*."

I clasped my hands tightly.

"I have been very foolish, Roderick," I said. "Please lie still and rest. You must not die! You must get well for — for I love you so very much!"

His eyes were a bright feverish blue against his pale face and black beard.

"You will never leave me?" he asked uncertainly. "You have left Brackenthorpe and Haughton and feel no regret?"

"Nothing matters but your recovery," I assured him softly. Impulsively I bent over the bed and touched his bearded cheek with the back of my hand. "Get better quickly, Roderick. When you are well you must tell me you forgive me for my obsession with Brackenthorpe. You were right — bricks and mortar did stand between us."

My eyes were filled with unshed tears when I saw the wondering look on his face. Then before I could say more he was asleep again.

Mistress Moore seemed satisfied with her son's condition after I had visited him and assured me that he would recover his health. I could have wept when she told me I had given him back the will to live. At last I stood convinced of his love and need for me.

In spite of my protests his mother

made me rest and to my shocked amazement I slept for a whole day. When I awoke, hungry but refreshed, I was permitted to go again to Roderick's secret chamber. We talked for long unchaperoned hours, exchanging our thoughts and hopes and exchanging also words of love which neither of us had ever thought to utter.

All that marred our new-found happiness was the fear of another unfriendly visit by Roundheads. I learned that on the last occasion, Mistress Moore had commanded her household to resist — with the result that many of her servants and valued friends had perished in this attempt to preserve Moorend for its absent master. Roderick had returned, barely alive, when the Roundheads had left and still knew nothing of what had taken place. At his mother's plea I took on the task of telling him when I thought him well enough to support the shock.

He seemed satisfied that I had

put both Brackenthorpe and Edmund behind me and listened gravely when I told him of the proposal of marriage I had received from Captain Hardcastle. I told him everything for there were no secrets between us now.

Late in September word arrived of Roderick's commander. Prince Rupert had been holding the city of Bristol for the King. Bristol was now in the hands of Parliament and royalists in the south of England were all fleeing or surrendering.

"The King's cause is lost," said Roderick when he heard this news. "Even if I were in full health I could now do nothing." Bitterly he added: "How can I rejoin my company if they have fled?"

Deeply afraid, I said nothing. I had hoped Roderick would put his days of soldiering behind him. I had not dreamed he held to the hope that he might still fight in the Prince's company. Even if he did not fight his sympathies must be well known to the enemy. Moorend had been attacked once. Roderick would never give up his convictions and bow the knee to Parliament. Edmund Haughton had turned his coat to support the winning side. I was both proud and sad to acknowledge that Roderick would die rather than do as Edmund had done.

17

RODERICK and I were married at the end of September. We found new happiness together despite the fear that the arrival of the enemy was imminent. The fact that we were undisturbed lulled us into a sense of security and we hoped that Parliament had forgotten Moorend. After all, what would the soldiers gain if they came to attack?

One morning in October I left the grounds accompanied only by William. We were on foot and did not intend to wander far. Our aim was to fill our baskets with hazelnuts and blackberries, both of which grew in profusion outside the walls. The morning was pleasantly warm and the fruit and nuts were plentiful. All was quiet and peaceful on the edge of the moor until suddenly two horsemen were upon us. They dismounted quickly, one to overpower William, the other to stand before me.

"Well met, Mistress Beth!" said Jonas Hardcastle harshly.

He was in full parliamentary uniform as was the soldier holding poor William. When he motioned me away and out of earshot of the others I began to tremble with fear.

"I had not thought to see you here, sir," I whispered.

He gave me an odd glance.

"You left Brackenthorpe secretly and without farewell. Young Haughton is very bitter against you. He guessed you would come here."

I saw the not unkindly look on Hardcastle's face, took a deep breath and threw myself on his mercy.

"Sir, I could not stay at Brackenthorpe. You tried to be kind to me but I dared not tell you the truth. How could I tell you that my heart was given to a royalist — to an enemy of yours?" I straightened my shoulders. "Roderick Moore is now my husband. I used you ill, sir, and will not ask your forgiveness."

He gave a heavy sigh.

"You have chosen the side of the vanquished, mistress," he said. "This strife is almost over. What would you have me do? My men are down in Skipton and a word from me would have them storming the walls of Moorend. Do you expect me to turn them aside and go against my own convictions?"

"I will not plead with you, sir," I said proudly. "If you attack my home you will find only women and servants and my — my husband, who is not yet recovered from wounds received in battle. Attack if you must but it will be a hollow victory."

"You refused the chance to possess Brackenthorpe and you refused the protection of my name, mistress," said Jonas Hardcastle reflectively. "I cannot understand you at all but I do not wish you harm. Go back into the house. I will lead my men south of here and leave you in peace. Go — surely you trust my word? But do not expect any further protection now that you have chosen to be my enemy."

"Sir — we are not enemies, you and I," I said unhappily. Impulsively I held out my hand. "Good-bye, sir, and thank you."

Neither of us had mentioned Kate. Either she had not spoken to him — had not accused me — or he had chosen to dismiss her spite. William and I set off back towards Moorend, nuts and berries forgotten. When once I turned my head, Jonas Hardcastle raised a hand in salute. Gratefully I waved back, then urged the dumbfounded William through the gates and into the safety of Moorend's courtyard.

"Mistress, he let us go!" gasped William.

"Yes," I said wearily, feeling drained of strength.

My feet dragged as I went to interrupt Roderick in his calculations of our household accounts. He listened to me gravely.

"Poor Beth," he said, putting an arm about my shaking shoulders. "He must have loved you more than you knew."

Roderick's mother would not be convinced of Hardcastle's sincerity.

"Do you tell me we must trust the word of an enemy?" she said incredulously. "It's all too likely that he will betray your trust, child. Even now he must be marshalling his men to attack."

★ ★ ★

A party of Roundhead soldiers arrived at Moorend on the afternoon of the following day and I stared in disbelief, aghast and saddened that Captain Hardcastle should have broken his word.

The gates had been secured but it was evident that they would not hold for long against a determined onslaught. Sick with apprehension, I listened to the shouts and demand for entry. The courtyard was empty and I could see no one ready to defend the house. Dully I stood at the partly-open main door, waiting for the gates to burst open. I fell back in alarm when a musket-shot hit the flagstones not far away and stone chippings struck the door beside me.

"Beth!" Roderick was at my side. He slammed the door and dropped the wooden bar in place. "Come, love," he urged, hauling me from the hall and into the next room. "Come, we're to hide down in the secret chamber. The enemy will find no horses. They are hidden down by the tarn." He paused with a gasp, pressing a hand to his chest. "Hurry, love! I thought you safe below with my mother and came in search when she had not seen you."

"But — shouldn't we fight?" I muttered. "Oh, I trusted Captain Hardcastle but your mother was right! He has attacked after all."

Roderick gave another gasp of pain

as we reached the tapestried wall and I forgot everything except that he was hurt and unfit for this exertion.

"Go down first, love," I said remorsefully. "I should not have made you come up in search of me. You are still not recovered."

With a grimace he obeyed and I was halfway through the secret aperture in his wake when I heard the door of the room burst open and the clatter of feet as someone entered. Hastily I pushed at the stonework to close up our place of retreat. To my alarm the stone would not move. The skirt of my gown was caught between the stones. Biting my lip, ignoring the ice-cold perspiration forming on my brow, I pulled at the cloth and tore my nails vainly on the rough stone. In my struggle I must have touched the tapestry, causing it to move and betray my presence, for feet were approaching rapidly. When a voice spoke softly in my ear I almost swooned with terror.

"The rest are hidden? Good — now

you must join them, child." It was Captain Hardcastle and I shrank from him, unable to believe he meant no harm. He saw how the cloth was caught and began to pull with me at the stubborn fabric. "Believe me, this attack was none of my doing," he muttered as he worked at freeing the trapped gown. "It was Braddock. I came in the hope of warning you first." At last the stone began to move. "God go with you, Beth," said Hardcastle. Then, as I gazed wide-eyed through the narrowing gap, I heard him shout to men now entering the room. "Nothing here — just solid wall behind this tapestry. I'd guess they've fled the house."

Shuddering with reaction, I leaned for a long moment against the cold rough stone of the stairway. I could no longer hear any sound from the room where the soldiers were. Half-falling in the darkness, I went down the stairs, to hurl myself weeping into Roderick's waiting arms. Stumbling over my words, I told him the way in which Jonas Hardcastle had kept his word.

"You were right, Roderick," I wept. "He must have loved me."

"As do we all, Beth," reassured my husband. "We must not let your captain's generous gesture go for naught. We will all stay hidden here until the soldiers leave the house. Later, when it is safe and I am fit to travel, we too must leave."

"Leave? Leave Moorend?" I asked in tearful bewilderment.

"Yes," said Roderick firmly against my hair. "I'll not have you make another Brackenthorpe of it, Beth! Bricks and mortar matter little against our own safety. If we stay here and cling to Moorend we will live in dread and fear. I will never relinquish my belief in my King's cause! But I will not let my belief make fugitives of us all. Perhaps one day we will come back. Do not look so downcast, Beth!"

We saw no more of the Roundheads and spent the winter quietly. Roderick grew stronger and more his old self with the passing of the weeks and I found that I could accept the necessity of leaving Moorend after all. It was spring of the next year before Roderick deemed the time ripe for us to disguise ourselves as poor travellers and begin the journey to the south of England in the hope of taking ship for France.

I quelled the urge to suggest that we call at Brackenthorpe. In spite of everything I would have liked to have bidden Edmund goodbye. However I held my tongue. Nothing mattered but our safe arrival in France. It was not really so very difficult for me to bid farewell to my homeland. Inwardly I was convinced that I would see England again. Time would pass, I assured myself, and with it must pass this present strife.

Thinking back on those occasions

when the Dream had been upon me, I realised I had only been *truly* misled by its message when I thought Roderick to be dead. Perhaps before many months elapsed I would have a vision of our homeland safe from oppression. I knew that if we did return I would never again make the foolish error of prizing a mere house above all else. Whatever might be in store, I knew the future must be secure with Roderick. In him I had found my destiny.

THE END

A YOUNG MAN'S FANCY
Nancy Bell

Six people get together for reasons of their own, and the result is one of misunderstanding, suspicion and mounting tension.

THE WISDOM OF LOVE
Janey Blair

Barbie meets Louis and receives flattering proposals, but her reawakened affection for Jonah develops into an overwhelming passion.

MIRAGE IN THE MOONLIGHT
Mandy Brown

En route to an island to be secretary to a multi-millionaire, Heather's stubborn loyalty to her former flatmate plunges her into a grim hazard.

WITH SOMEBODY ELSE
Theresa Charles

Rosamond sets off for Cornwall with Hugo to meet his family, blissfully unaware of the shocks in store for her.

A SUMMER FOR STRANGERS
Claire Hamilton

Because she had lost her job, her flat and she had no money, Tabitha agreed to pose as Adam's future wife although she believed the scheme to be deceitful and cruel.

VILLA OF SINGING WATER
Angela Petron

The disquieting incidents that occurred at the Vatican and the Colosseum did not trouble Jan at first, but then they became increasingly unpleasant and alarming.

DOCTOR NAPIER'S NURSE
Pauline Ash

When cousins Midge and Derry are entered as probationer nurses on the same day but at different hospitals they agree to exchange identities.

A GIRL LIKE JULIE
Louise Ellis

Caroline absolutely adored Hugh Barrington, but then Julie Crane came into their lives. Julie was the kind of girl who attracts men without even trying.

COUNTRY DOCTOR
Paula Lindsay

When Evan Richmond bought a practice in a remote country village he did not realise that a casual encounter would lead to the loss of his heart.

ENCORE
Helga Moray

Craig and Janet realise that their true happiness lies with each other, but it is only under traumatic circumstances that they can be reunited.

NICOLETTE
Ivy Preston

When Grant Alston came back into her life, Nicolette was faced with a dilemma. Should she follow the path of duty or the path of love?

THE GOLDEN PUMA
Margaret Way

Catherine's time was spent looking after her father's Queensland farm. But what life was there without David, who wasn't interested in her?

HOSPITAL BY THE LAKE
Anne Durham

Nurse Marguerite Ingleby was always ready to become personally involved with her patients, to the despair of Brian Field, the Senior Surgical Registrar, who loved her.

VALLEY OF CONFLICT
David Farrell

Isolated in a hostel in the French Alps, Ann Russell sees her fiancé being seduced by a young girl. Then comes the avalanche that imperils their lives.

NURSE'S CHOICE
Peggy Gaddis

A proposal of marriage from the incredibly handsome and wealthy Reagan was enough to upset any girl — and Brooke Martin was no exception.

A DANGEROUS MAN
Anne Goring

Photographer Polly Burton was on safari in Mombasa when she met enigmatic Leon Hammond. But unpredictability was the name of the game where Leon was concerned.

PRECIOUS INHERITANCE
Joan Moules

Karen's new life working for an authoress took her from Sussex to a foreign airstrip and a kidnapping; to a real life adventure as gripping as any in the books she typed.

VISION OF LOVE
Grace Richmond

When Kathy takes over the rundown country kennels she finds Alec Stinton, a local vet, very helpful. But their friendship arouses bitter jealousy and a tragedy seems inevitable.

CRUSADING NURSE
Jane Converse

It was handsome Dr. Corbett who opened Nurse Susan Leighton's eyes and who set her off on a lonely crusade against some powerful enemies and a shattering struggle against the man she loved.

WILD ENCHANTMENT
Christina Green

Rowan's agreeable new boss had a dream of creating a famous perfume using her precious Silverstar, but Rowan's plans were very different.

DESERT ROMANCE
Irene Ord

Sally agrees to take her sister Pam's place as La Chartreuse the dancer, but she finds out there is more to it than dyeing her hair red and looking like her sister.

HEART OF ICE
Marie Sidney

How was January to know that not only would the warmth of the Swiss people thaw out her frozen heart, but that she too would play her part in helping someone to live again?

LUCKY IN LOVE
Margaret Wood

Companion-secretary to wealthy gambler Laura Duxford, who lived in Monaco, seemed to Melanie a fabulous job. Especially as Melanie had already lost her heart to Laura's son, Julian.

NURSE TO PRINCESS JASMINE
Lilian Woodward

Nick's surgeon brother, Tom, performs an operation on an Arabian princess, and she invites Tom, Nick and his fiancé to Omander, where a web of deceit and intrigue closes about them.

THE WAYWARD HEART
Eileen Barry

Disaster-prone Katherine's nickname was "Kate Calamity", but her boss went too far with an outrageous proposal, which because of her latest disaster, she could not refuse.

FOUR WEEKS IN WINTER
Jane Donnelly

Tessa wasn't looking forward to meeting Paul Mellor again — she had made a fool of herself over him once before. But was Orme Jared's solution to her problem likely to be the right one?

SURGERY BY THE SEA
Sheila Douglas

Medical student Meg hadn't really wanted to go and work with a G.P. on the Welsh coast although the job had its compensations. But Owen Roberts was certainly not one of them!

HEAVEN IS HIGH
Anne Hampson

The new heir to the Manor of Marbeck had been found. But it was rather unfortunate that when he arrived unexpectedly he found an uninvited guest, complete with stetson and high boots.

LOVE WILL COME
Sarah Devon

June Baker's boss was not really her idea of her ideal man, but when she went from third typist to boss's secretary overnight she began to change her mind.

ESCAPE TO ROMANCE
Kay Winchester

Oliver and Jean first met on Swale Island. They were both trying to begin their lives afresh, but neither had bargained for complications from the past.